MERFOLK'S MATE

DRAKE LAMARQUE

GREY KELPIE STUDIO

ISBN paperback edition 978-0-473-50698-8

Cover by Sarah Loch of Purple Dragon Design

www.purpledragondesign.com

Printed in United States of America via Kindle Direct Publishing

Published by Grey Kelpie Studio

DEDICATION

Dedicated to all my readers, and to the awesome and friendly MM Romance authors who have made the community so friendly. Love to all of you.

CHAPTER ONE - IN WHICH COMMUNICATIONS ARE EXCHANGED

The Splintered Isles

The waves lapped at the rocks, which were jagged as so many of the rocks were on the Splintered Isles. Solomon wondered, not for the first time, what the island cluster would have been called if the rocks were smooth.

Cursed Isles maybe, or if they'd been discovered by someone as sharp as myself, the Source of Power Isles.

He inhaled the early morning air. No dew here on the beach, only the bright morning sunshine and the sea spray, coating his lips with salt. He let his breath out deliberately, calling on the power within him, akin to when he was a child and his mother would send him to draw water out of the well in the back of their house. Dipping down, drawing out the water.

Then he felt the well deepen, and he drew magic from the island itself.

If Tate had known the true nature of this place, there's no way he'd have left me here.

The magic flowed up from the sand, from the water, into his

body and, as it took hold, he began to see it - flowing like blood through the veins of the landscape and into him.

Solomon rolled his shoulders, smiling as his neck cracked, the bones of his spine settling into place. The magic, which seemed to come from something under the island, perhaps inside the Earth itself, always reset his body when he summoned it in this way. It was as refreshing as a swim in the ocean, or a good night's sleep, and it fortified him with what he thought of as the true essence of nature.

Clad only in close-fitting black trousers that had served him for many years, he held in one hand a braided cord with several knots in it. Loosely, in his other hand, an amulet dangled, one he'd constructed himself out of a shell and a stone found in a rock pool under the full moon.

Although, I'll hardly need the amulet today. Nature's essence is flowing strong enough.

He moved forward, past the hard-packed damp sand and into the lapping waves, until he was almost knee-deep in the clear Caribbean water.

Closing his eyes once more he inhaled and focused the energy coursing through him into a single point. Where was the Grey Kelpie?

Where was the ship that held Tate - lying Tate. Tate the bloody. The thief. The betrayer. The false lover who played sweet and then turned on a whim, quicker than the prevailing winds.

There.

He slipped the amulet around his neck to amplify his power - and took one end of the cord in each hand. Fingers working fast as he spoke words of power, Solomon narrowed in on the position of the hated ship on the ocean and summoned a fog to swamp it.

It would take some hours to reach the ship - a fog didn't just coalesce out of nowhere and nothing, even for someone like Solomon - harnessing the power of the Isles.

He knotted the cord - binding the Kelpie to the fog, setting his intention for the fog to trap them and force them in place.

He felt the wind resist him, the weather systems, which Solomon imagined as capricious spirits, bucking against his request to act counter to the natural way of things. Gritting his teeth he tied another knot in the cord and shoved his power into the binding, speaking a word of power that burned his tongue and scorched his throat.

That was enough. The weather spirits - such as they were - settled under his yoke and he could feel in his toes, half-buried in the sand, that his will would be obeyed.

He opened his eyes and cleared his throat, which felt rough and raw after that word.

I shouldn't have had to invoke quite so much power just for a fog. I wonder if other forces are moving against me somehow? Or perhaps it's simply the weather itself. A clear, fine day doesn't give easily to mist.

Pocketing the knotted cord he rinsed his hands in seawater before heading back up the beach, up the stone staircase he'd fashioned over the years to his main living area. He took a seat on the chaise - the same one he'd kept that whelp, Gideon, on - and let his body drop into a meditative state.

In order to reach another's dreams, he had to be close to dreams himself.

But he shouldn't have thought of Gideon. Thinking of him stirred anger and resentment that was counterproductive. That simpering, stupid dandy who had whined and cowered... but then tried to talk to Solomon as if he could be reasoned with. As if he didn't have every cause to pursue revenge.

As if there's something inside me that needs saving.

Solomon stood with an aggravated growl and stalked out to

the observation platform he'd fashioned in the largest part of the cave system he inhabited. From there he could see the sunlight glittering on the blue waves, the horizon beckoning him, although never enough to tempt him from here in his seat of power.

He sat with his legs dangling and let the movement of the waves soothe him. Anger was good, it could fuel him a lot of the time, but for meditation he needed to become as fluid, as slippery as water. Let the emotions wash over him and then away, leave them behind for the absolute calm he needed.

As he relaxed, gazing at the lights on the water and feeling his connection to the Earth beneath them, his breathing became slow, and his body ceased moving. His eyes didn't blink, and even the gentle breeze blowing his hair into his eyes didn't cause a stir.

Several hours passed with Solomon in this position, until he finally took a deep, rasping breath and came back to himself.

A dream sent in the middle of the day, implanted in another's mind... the most receptive mind in the Naval crew, I believe. Lucky for me he was in the area at all.

But Solomon wasn't particularly surprised by this stroke of luck. Lately, something had been telling him - perhaps it was the stars or the universe itself - that his plans would soon come to fruition.

He had just had Tate in his grasp after all, not long ago at all. He'd seen the man, wrapped in Solomon's own chains, close enough that Solomon could have bitten him and tasted his blood - but of course Gideon had interfered.

When Solomon had woken, hours later, he'd pieced together something of the events. Somehow Gideon had enslaved one of the merfolk and used that voice to still Solomon and save the crew.

It had worked, but it was only a temporary reprieve. Solomon's thirst was whetted now, and if the stars were to be believed then his plans in motion would work, and soon the Navy would ship Tate almost directly to him.

Well. They'd sail past his Islands, anyway, and then it was a simple matter of a wave or a storm, and Tate would be in Solomon's hands again. Under his thumb and squirming.

Maybe Solomon would take Gideon too, just so he would watch Tate's anguish as Gideon was tortured.

If he cared about him so much - which Solomon's spell indicated he did - it could be a fine way to pass some time, break Tate to his will.

The thought made Solomon smile. It was certainly something to consider.

He went to lie down in bed, exhausted from the spells he'd performed and went to sleep smiling, imagining the cries of pain.

CHAPTER TWO - IN WHICH GIDEON SPEAKS WITH CAPTAIN THORNTON

HMS TRINITY ROYAL

Zack, an ensign in the Royal Navy, led me to the Captain's cabin. It felt somewhat like being led to the gallows, although I was relatively confident that they believed I'd been kidnapped and not actively engaging in piracy.

Which I absolutely had been. I'd not killed any of the slavers, but I had been part of the crew overwhelming them. Afterwards, I counted out the spoils from the slaver ship the Kelpie liberated. If they found that out it would be the gallows for sure, although, perhaps Father would pay someone off to get me a pardon.

Father would almost certainly pay for a pardon for me.

"Are you sure you don't want to rest up a bit more before you see the Captain?" Zack asked, turning back to look at me, his forehead crinkling in a surprisingly concerned way.

"I'm fine," I said. Although truth to tell I was feeling lightheaded and utterly dreading the conversation I was about to have with Thornton. "Please, you didn't tell me. Uh, how long ago did you take the Grey Kelpie?"

Zack's eyes widened, almost shining with the memory of it. "Day before yesterday," he said. "Ship's doctor gave you some laudanum to help you sleep off the worst of the hurts those brutes did to you. The dose's worn off now obviously, but he thought you might still feel sore or maybe a little faint."

I bit my tongue on my response. But I'm sure I flushed red with the sudden anger I was suppressing. Hopefully Zack would interpret it as embarrassment.

Referring to them as those brutes. The loves of my life, would be more accurate.

I nodded as Zack eyed me, then he was on the move again. We arrived at the Captain's door after passing several Naval officers who all took long, lingering looks at me. Well, they'd all seen the state I'd been in when they took the Kelpie.

Naked, bound by the wrists to the yardarm of the main mast, back red with the welts of the whipping Ezra had given me, fucked out and exhausted from it. Not to mention, I was almost hysterical from pleasure and pain and the sheer overwhelming effect my lovers had on my body and my emotional state.

I know very well how it must've looked to someone who didn't understand.

Zack knocked on the door and waited, shifting from one foot to the other and looking every inch the nervous ensign who feared his Captain.

A cold, familiar voice called out within.

"Enter."

Zack opened the door and went in first, seeming to suck up his fear and square his shoulders.

I straightened my spine, lifted my chin and summoned all the dignity I could muster. It wasn't much, but when I thought back to my preparatory school deportment master, and the fact that I was, after all, my father's son, and that these men had interrupted an exceptionally wonderful time I'd been enjoying with my four lovers, only two of whom were properly human.

Well, I felt a little more confident after thinking about that.

I walked in and moved to stand beside Zack, tipping my chin up and letting my face relax utterly.

Thornton was a tall, thin, pinched looking man. He probably wasn't as old as he looked, as years of sun had wrinkled his face. His insistence on wearing the powdered white wig aged him even further under his beetled brows.

On reflection, I expected he was younger than my Father. Putting him a little older than Tate. He had eyes of palest blue, which seemed almost uncanny now that I was regarding them in the dim light of his cabin.

He had a definite sense of gravitas to him. An aura of authority that my instincts told me I should submit to. I swallowed, looking at him and trying to remember he was my enemy in this case.

"Captain, this is Gideon Keene, Sir. He's awake and in his faculties."

"So I see," Thornton said. He set down a pair of spectacles on the desk in front of him and folded his arms. "It's been a while since we last spoke, Master Keene."

I felt my confidence waver further under the cold steel stare. I took a long, slow breath.

"It has indeed, Captain," I said. "I hope you've been well." This was a conversation for which I'd need all my etiquette training. I swallowed and tried to put myself at ease, relaxing to allow my skills and my training to come back to me.

"Very well, thank you," he said. "I expect the first order of business is that you'd like to thank me for the, uh, rescue."

At those words, I had to resist the urge to spit at him. It flared up inside me, hot and sudden. I quelled it with another breath and intentionally did not grit my teeth together. I let my training take over and replied as smoothly as I could.

"Indeed, thank you, Captain," I said, trying not to wince as my voice sounded obviously stiff. "Although I wasn't actually in need of it."

Thornton scoffed and raised his eyebrows. "They had you bound, whipped and... worse." He said, picking up a handkerchief and dabbing at his forehead. It was sweaty and hot under the ridiculous wig he wore.

Or, I supposed, maybe it was the impropriety he was referring to that had him perspiring. He must've seen every single inch of my naked body, and those of my lovers come to that.

I wonder what he thinks of me?

"I don't know what bribe those pirates have offered you, but there's no point pretending."

"They didn't offer me any bribes," I said, fighting to keep my voice even.

I tore my gaze from his, trying to get the sudden, powerful and unwelcome flare of anger under control.

I reflected that when I had walked in, this room had felt sombre, vast and intimidating. Now, with fresh eyes, I saw that Thornton's cabin was smaller than Tate's, which gave me some amount of satisfaction. He had a tiny cot built into the wall, and a desk barely large enough to hold his ledger. He had a stack of papers and an inkwell in front of him, and a curious little wooden box.

It was far too large to be a snuff box, which would suggest it was for either jewelry or bullets. I couldn't imagine the Captain wearing a lot of jewelry.

"Indeed," Captain said. "Then I must admit I'm utterly confused about why you insist you weren't kidnapped, when you patently were."

"I ran away," I said. My eye was caught by the box on his desk, there was something about it that intrigued me. With an effort I met his gaze again. "Please, you must understand, I ran away from my Father's house to make my own way in the world, and the Grey Kelpie is the ship I joined."

Beside me, Zack made a surprised noise and Thornton cut his eyes at him sharply. Zack shuffled and was silent.

"You expect me to believe you ran away from home, and

accidentally joined a pirate ship?" His tone dripped with a vast amount of condescension and I realised arguing my cause was pointless.

Like Father, this man would never, could never understand what had happened.

"Well, when you put it like that it does sound rather... outlandish," I said, dropping my eyes.

I shifted on my feet.

Perhaps, in this situation, I'd be better suited to playing the simpleton, the ridiculous fool son he no doubt already thought I was. I would pretend to be grateful and not raise any doubts in his mind. If he knew that I had no intention of sitting still and letting them sail Tate and Ezra to their dooms he might lock me up, too. I had to keep suspicion off me.

"It does. I'm glad you agree," Thornton said. He stood up from his desk and took a deep breath before strolling towards me. "At any rate, I'm glad to see you up and about. The Governor, your father, will be very pleased to hear of your progress, I'm sure."

"Hear of my progress?" I cleared my throat and blinked at Thornton, making my eyes as large and guileless as I knew how to do. "You can't possibly be sending courier pigeons this far all the way to Kingston."

"No, of course not." Thornton placed his hand on my shoulder and gave it what he probably thought of as a fatherly squeeze. I suppressed a shudder and kept my expression mild.

"Then how could he possibly be kept informed of your news?" I blinked and tilted my head as if I had no thoughts in there at all.

"We have our ways. Now, Master Keene, I'm sure you need more rest. How about you come and have tea with me tomorrow and we can talk further?" His fingers moved, slowly rubbing my shoulder and making my skin crawl.

"Of course," I said. My eyes slipped back to the wooden box

on his desk - something about it was almost calling to me. I shrugged my shoulders, hoping he'd take the hint and let go of me. "Just, uh, one more thing, if I may be so bold as to make a request?"

"What is it?"

"The pirates, uh, Bloody Tate and the Shearwater. Are they - are they being kept on this ship?" I knew they were, Ensign Zack had told me as much, but I wanted him to think I was clueless as possible.

"They are. They are both locked safely away in the brig where they can't get at you. You're quite safe with us, Gideon. Now, I'd rather while you convalesce you stay mostly confined to the infirmary, if you don't mind," Thornton said. He turned me with his hand on my shoulder and guided me back towards the door. "Just so you can recover, and stay out of the way of the men, you understand."

"I'm not a prisoner am I?" I asked, genuine surprise tingeing my voice.

"No, of course not, you're our guest. I just don't want you distracting the crew with any wild stories or getting yourself worked up unnecessarily. We'll have you back to Kingston within a fortnight, so you don't need to worry yourself. If you need anything at all, Ensign Jacobs here will see to it. He'll bring you your meals and so on."

I felt my freedom rapidly slipping away and stopped at the door, took a quick breath. "Please, Captain. If I might be allowed, would it be possible for me to have some time up on deck during the day? I'll stay quite out of the way, I just. I just think the sea air would be beneficial to my recovery."

Thornton eyed me with his severe gaze, and then nodded.

"Very well. An hour at the start of the first dog watch, you can stroll the deck. But mind you keep out of the way and if there's any alarm or drill it will take precedent and you'll return immediately to the infirmary."

"Yes, Captain, thank you." I said.

Zack and I left the cabin and made our way back towards the
infirmary but this time I was much more alert. This was the ship
I served on in my ill-fated year in the Navy, which meant I knew
where the brig was. The trick would be finding a way down
there with no one noticing.

Ensign Zack was quiet until we got back to the infirmary.

"Thank you for escorting me," I said. I sighed as I sat down
on the cot. "And for explaining things."

"That was marvelous, what you did back there," Zack said,
softly. His eyes were wide and shining.

"It was?"

"Aye, you changed your story so neatly, and you made it
seem like it was because you was agreeing with him," he said.

Something caught in my chest. "I didn't-" I said hurriedly. I
couldn't have Zack suspicious of me and it sounded as if he'd
seen right through my ploy. "I wasn't hiding anything, I just-"

"Oh, no, it's all right." Zack shut the door, moved forward
and gave me a conspiratorial smile. "I'll not tell anyone. I just
thought you handled Thornton so beautifully, I wondered if you
could teach me a thing or two."

"Oh." I stifled a surprised laugh. "Teach you what? How to
lie?"

"Uh, no, I already know how to lie," Zack said. His voice was
low, and he moved closer towards me, and I felt as if we were
suddenly conspirators together. "But the manners and the... how
do you call it, like, talking about something without actually
talking about it."

I tilted my head. "I suppose you are referring to subtext?"

Zack shook his head and shrugged. "I dunno, you tell me."
He had a pleasant Scottish lilt to his voice and I felt myself
warming to him.

I inhaled, trying to think it all through before I replied. I sat down on the bed and ran my hands through my hair. It was getting longer, and I sort of liked it that way. It marked me as different from all the Naval men with their shorter cropped hair.

Zack wanted something from me, which was a good sign. If he wanted something from me there was a chance I could leverage that for something I needed.

"Listen," I said, looking down, trying to demur a bit so that he wouldn't think I was up to any kind of trickery. "I'd really like to help you, but I'm not sure if there's anything I could teach you."

Zack folded his arms and barked out an impressed laugh. "Amazing, you're a complete natural."

I didn't know whether to be flattered or insulted, but my nerves were on edge - every time I thought about my situation my stomach knotted further. I had to exploit this opportunity. I looked into Zack's eyes and gave him my best pleading look. It wasn't hard, I very, very much wanted to check that Tate and Ezra and whoever else they had down there from the Kelpie was alive and unharmed.

"Listen, do you think, is there any chance... that you could arrange to get me down to the brig?"

Zack raised his eyebrows and tilted his head slightly. "Now, I know you changed your story back there with the Captain, but why would you want to visit the brig? What's really going on with you and those pirates?"

"I told you already," I said, rolling my eyes and sighing. "I wasn't kidnapped. Listen, if you can get me down there, if you give me some time to speak to them, then I'll help you. I'll tell you anything you want to know."

Zack huffed a little and nodded. "Right, all right. Let me... it's best if we go at the change of watch," he said, finally. "People will be moving around, busy with their own things, like."

I was surprised and pleased that Zack had agreed so readily.

A coil of my own suspicion unfurled in my stomach. Whatever Zack thought he could learn from me, he must be valuing it highly. But it didn't matter. I'd get to see my lovers, that was the most important thing for the moment.

"All right. Good, so, uh, how long is that?"

"Soon," Zack said. "I'll go down there now, scope out what the guard is like below and come and get you when it's time. All right?"

I nodded. "Thank you, really. I appreciate it."

Zack left with a little, uncertain salute and I had to smile - I wasn't at all sure what to make of Zack, except that something in me liked him.

I hope I can trust him. I'm certain I can't pretend I don't care about my lovers when I see them, whatever perceived skill in deception Zack thinks I have.

He'll soon know the truth of what I've said.

CHAPTER THREE - IN WHICH TATE
AND EZRA ARE VISITED AND TRUTHS
ARE SHARED

Zack knocked before letting himself in and I found my
heart leaping a little at the thought of company.

He'd been gone a good few hours, and I'd quickly run out of
things to do in the small infirmary. I had cleaned my face with
the jug of water and combed out my hair as best I could with my
fingers.

There was nothing to read in the room, and I'd spent far too
long staring at the diagrams of the human body and learning
the names of the various bones of the skeleton.

I missed companionship. I was so used to having the full run
of the Kelpie - being able to approach people and receiving hugs
and kisses, my body felt cold and somehow... itchy with the
need to see someone I loved.

*I really have become spoiled, it's been a couple of hours and I'm
near crying for kisses from my lovers.*

No, it's not that bad, I just need someone to talk to.

Zack hardly counted as someone I loved, but he was
someone I could talk to at least.

I could have left the room, of course, my door wasn't locked
and I wasn't a prisoner, but I didn't want to be seen to be making
trouble. The less people noticing me the better, and besides,

Thornton had asked me to stay out of the way and I didn't want to catch his eye at all.

So I stayed put and paced the room, lay on my front on the cot to give my whipped back a rest, and sighed a lot, wishing the time would pass faster.

When Zack knocked on the door of the infirmary, I nearly leapt to my feet, ready to go.

"Is it time?"

"Yes," Zack said. His voice hushed again. "They don't have a regular guard, on account of being locked in the brig, and the Captain splitting the crew between this ship and the pirate one. So, come on, we can go look at them."

The Captain had split the crew between the two ships? That was good information to have.

"Right, thank you, please lead on."

Zack turned and I followed.

Suddenly nervous, I ran my hands through my hair, making sure it wasn't standing up in a strange way or tangled. My stomach filled with dread but it was mixed with excited butterflies.

I hated the thought of them locked up like that, and chained as well... but I was so excited to see them again. I tugged at the hem of my shirt and swallowed.

We trod the familiar corridors and down to the brig - not that I'd had cause to be down here much as a Naval recruit. The brig was dark and unpleasantly musty smelling, situated at the aft of the ship, on a level that was largely storage and supplies.

"Just there," Zack said. He gestured at the barred cell doors and stood to one side, hovering near the access way, I suspected to waylay any other sailors.

I walked towards the cell doors, swallowing nervously.

Ezra sat with his back to the wall, head tilted back, his eyes closed. His hair was a mess, he was unshaven and he wore a plain linen shirt like mine and an ill-fitting pair of standard

16

issue Naval trousers. His hands rested in his lap, and I could see a thick chain leading from there to an iron loop on the wall.

Tate was dressed similarly, but he sat closer to the bars, cross legged on the floor of the cell. He looked up as I approached and his face broke into a huge smile, his eyes crinkling.

"Gideon! See, Ezra, I told you he was all right," Tate said. He kicked Ezra gently in the side.

Ezra's eyes snapped open and he got to his feet, moving towards the bars of the cell door.

"Gideon. Are you all right? Did they hurt you? If they've hurt you I swear by all the Gods -"

"Yes, I'm all right, no, they didn't hurt me, they've uh. Given me medical attention, and laudanum, a heavy dose I think. I only woke up this morning." I held up my wrist so he could see the bandaging covering the rope burns. Not that I needed it, but leaving that on seemed like a prudent way to continue my deception of seeming helpless and dull.

Tate stood and reached a hand out to me, instinctively I got as close as I could to the bars and reached through to squeeze his hand.

His fingers were cold, and the iron bars pressed against my body in an unpleasant fashion. My heart tugged with pain, feeling how cold he was but it was so good to touch him, it was like a strike of lightning through my arm and up into my body.

Tate's eyes widened as if he'd felt it too. I smiled, close to tears all of a sudden, and had to swallow hard to keep my emotions in check.

"We weren't sure what they'd have done to you, love," Tate said. "The Captains's very..." he looked behind me to Zack and then lowered his voice. "Strict."

"Yes, he is. He's..."

Ezra moved as close as he was able with the chain holding him back and I reached my other hand through the bars to touch his hand. His fingers closed on mine and my shoulders slumped, a little of the tension leaking out of my body.

"He's sailing us to Kingston as fast as the winds allow. The Kelpie's with us, they said. Part of the crew of this ship is over there."

Tate exhaled. "Well, I'm glad to hear they didn't sink her, anyway. How are the rest of the crew, Ora? Sagorika?"

"In the Kelpie's brig," I said. "Ora went overboard, I don't know about any of the others." My voice cracked a little, thinking of Zeb. He'd not been a human long at all, he wouldn't cope with being ordered around by a stranger. He'd fight, continue to fight.

"I'm sure he's fine," Tate said, as if reading my thoughts. "Zeb's a survivor."

"And what's *your* fate to be?" Ezra asked, raising an eyebrow. He was rubbing his forefinger back and forth over the back of my hand. Tate had threaded his fingers in mine and held tight.

My breath hitched in my chest. I turned my head to look at Zack, who was clearly trying not to look like he was listening in.

I was already holding hands with both of them, pressing myself bodily against the bars. I wonder what he'd make of it.

Ezra looked past me at Zack and twisted his mouth to the side. "Can we trust him?"

"I don't know, maybe. He got me down here to visit you secretly." I lowered my voice. "Thornton has promised to deliver me to my father, and get the reward payment. I... do not wish for that outcome. Father will have me married within a week."

Tate and Ezra exchanged a look that seemed to have a deeper meaning.

"Gideon, please. Don't do anything that puts yourself at risk, you're too precious," Tate said. He moved closer to the bars, hindered by the chains on his wrists but closer, so he could talk lower. "I know you'll be trying to think up some misguided escape plan but Ezra and I agreed we don't want you risking yourself for us."

I looked to Ezra who nodded his agreement and I shook my head in disbelief. "You may have agreed but I have not. I'll not let you be delivered to the gallows."

They exchanged another look and I shook my head. "Well, you can hardly stop me from trying whatever I like, anyway." I sighed. "Are they feeding you? Have you got enough water?"

"Aye, lad," Tate's expression softened. "We're all right."

"Got out of worse scrapes than this before," Ezra said, his light tone somewhat betrayed by the hoarse strain in his voice. "We'll be fine."

I frowned and squeezed both of their hands. "I love you both, and I'll get you out of this somehow. I swear it." I felt my throat close and my breath hitch and I closed my eyes against the tears that threatened to well up again.

Tate sighed, bent down and gently kissed the back of my hand.

Ezra squeezed my other hand and let go. "Look after yourself first, that's an order, pet," he growled. I was astounded that even while locked and chained in a dank brig, he could muster some sort of authority and give me a salacious thrill. One I had to instantly tamp down so as not to get distracted.

In fact, it strengthened my resolve to do something to break them out. I needed Ezra to show me just how much authority he had over me, and I needed that to happen in private.

"I'll look after myself," I said, nodding. "But I am determined to do whatever I can to look after you two as well."

"Master Keene," Zack said, raising his voice loud enough to carry over our murmuring. "We should get up on deck, it's the start of the first dog watch."

I sighed heavily and smiled sadly as Tate kissed the tips of my fingers. "I'll come back and visit as soon as I can. I love you, both of you."

"Love you, Gid," Tate said. He let go of my fingers. Ezra nodded and took a deep breath.

"Look after yourself, Gideon," he said, loud enough for Zack to overhear.

"I will."

With a feeling as if my heart was tearing itself in half, I pulled my hands back and turned away, swallowing a lump in my throat and trying to put on a blank expression for Zack's benefit.

Zack didn't say anything, just led the way out of the brig and up to the foredeck. His posture had a certain tension to it, but I was grateful he'd turned his back. It gave me a chance to wipe my eyes and gather myself together.

CHAPTER FOUR - IN WHICH SECRETS ARE SHARED

It was the first fresh air I'd had in days and I inhaled deeply, feeling the warmth of the sunshine on the deck under my bare feet. The sun was warm on my body but it felt as if my heart was still down in the brig, cold and contained.

It felt good to have the sun on my skin, and the smell of the salt in my nose, but what I really wanted was to see - there - the Grey Kelpie sailing nearby. Less than twenty paces away, if one could walk on the water.

I went to the side of the Trinity Royal and looked at it, letting my fear and concern wash over me. I felt the tears spill out and couldn't find it in me to care. Whatever Tate and Ezra had said, I knew I had to do something. There was no way I'd let Thornton take them to the gallows.

But I was at a loss for what to do on my own.

I could see men in Naval blues moving around on the deck of the Kelpie, adjusting the sails, swabbing the deck. The sight of their uniforms on the beloved ship was so incongruous it felt almost obscene.

I missed the ship, far more than I had ever missed my home in Kingston. The Kelpie was a place where I had found true happiness, where I had been able to live my true desires, ask for what I want and have it given to me, and in turn take care of those I loved.

That life was lost to me, or it might be...

I saw now how much of a clash there was between the life I'd had on the ship and how society operated. There was no way I could live in a place like Kingston and have multiple male lovers. We had so much freedom on the ship to do as we pleased, which wouldn't be tolerated elsewhere.

What kind of future did I have to look forward to?

If I couldn't get free of the Trinity Royal - God forbid - it would be back at my Father's house, where he'd no doubt lock me in my room until he could marry me to some rich girl and then he'd presumably give her the key to my room and not a lot would change.

Eventually, I'd take over Father's position and forget all the joy I'd had out at sea.

Or maybe it would just haunt me forever.

But, if I could get free of the Trinity, and free Ezra and Tate as well, somehow get us all back on the Kelpie together, what would that future hold? Continually running from the Royal fleet? Hoping that Solomon would lose interest and stop trying to destroy Tate?

How could we possibly overcome such determined enemies?

I used my sleeve to wipe my eyes and sighed. Staring out at the Kelpie and just wishing wasn't going to achieve anything. I had to pull myself together.

I had to start thinking about practical steps to take. Instead I was wasting time daydreaming and making myself feel wretched.

"Are you all right?"

I turned to see Zack watching me from a couple of feet away. I had all but forgotten he'd be keeping an eye on me, too lost in my own maelstrom of thoughts.

"No," I said, without thinking. Perhaps I should have given him a pat answer and said I was fine, but I couldn't find it in my heart to lie about this to Zack. He glanced at the sailors working nearby.

"Perhaps I ought to take you back down to the infirmary, Master Keene?" He raised his eyebrows significantly.

The nearest few sailors were watching us while they worked, their hands moving slower than before. I was sure I'd been the talk of the ship already, and I flushed, humiliated.

Here I was giving them more to gossip about.

"Please call me Gideon," I said. I followed him back to the tiny cabin that would be my home for the foreseeable future, feeling humiliated and sad.

Once we were inside, Zack took one of my hands. Startled, I snatched it back and stepped away from him.

"What's the meaning of this?" I asked. Suddenly afraid that because Zack had seen me with Tate and Ezra, he thought I'd be willing to sleep with him as well. I was in far too much anguish to even consider such a thing - and felt almost no attraction to him whatsoever.

"Please, Gideon, I didn't mean anything, just wanted to hold your hand," Zack said. He checked that the door behind him was shut fast and took a step towards me. "You said that you weren't kidnapped. Will you tell me what really happened?"

I sat down on the bed and folded my arms. "Is this so you can share my tall stories with the other sailors? I'm sure all of you are sharing stories of how you found me, what I must have been through and making fun."

"No," Zack huffed. "I thought you and I had a deal."

"We do, I'll tutor you in conversational arts and you will allow me to visit the brig." I eyed him warily. Uncertain what else he wanted to know.

"I... I suppose there's no reason for you to trust me," Zack said.

"You're correct," I said. "And honestly, I'm sorry for it. You seem to be a decent sort of fellow, and Lord knows I could use an ally on this ship. But I don't want to be made a laughing stock."

"The fact is," Zack said. He paused, pushed a hand through his hair and sighed. "Look, I'm in just as much danger of being a laughing stock on this ship as you are. If you're willing to hear me out, I think I can help."

I tilted my head, trying to puzzle out what he was saying to me. Zack was in danger of being a laughing stock? In what way?

Did he perhaps understand that I was in love with Tate and Ezra?

"I, uh, I..." I stammered.

The bells rang for a change of watch and Zack swore under his breath.

"I'm sorry, I have to go. I'll be back with your dinner after I've done my jobs for the day. Just... think about it all right?"

He gazed into my eyes, apparently unwilling to leave until I'd responded to his suggestion. "I'll, yes, of course I'll think about it," I said.

Zack flashed a smile - white teeth and a dimple in his cheek and then was gone. I was left to stew in my thoughts again.

As the minutes turned into hours I started to really hate the four walls of the cabin. I went to the door, opened it and looked out at the bare corridor, but I didn't venture further.

I absolutely have to play along for now. I must not draw any more attention to myself.

I went back into the room, sat on the bed, and tried to decipher what Zack had been trying to say.

After chasing his words and his expressions around my brain for a while I had to conclude that I didn't have enough information to guess.

Something inside me told me I could take a leap of faith

with Zack. Perhaps because he had shown me some modicum of kindness, perhaps simply because he had expressed that he too was hiding something. I decided to risk it, and ask for his help.

I tried to fall asleep to pass the time but I couldn't manage to drop off. I kept remembering that Tate and Ezra needed me, that they were locked up and in need of rescue.

My heart ached and my stomach knotted. I needed to be doing more, and instead I was lying still. It was impossible to bear, but without having a plan or understanding what Zack was offering, I couldn't plan anything.

"I'm going to run mad in this room," I said to the ceiling. I wished I had my mother's portrait to speak to. That always made me feel better. I hoped it was still in place in my old cabin on the Grey Kelpie.

Please, Mother, I could use some of your patience. I'm a mess of emotions and I don't know what to do. I want so much.

I sent the thought up like a prayer and closed my eyes against the tears that had welled up once more.

Gideon, my darling, I imagined her voice saying to me. *Just breathe. Breathe and wait. It will all turn out alright in the end.*

Had I imagined her voice saying that, or was it a memory?

Perhaps it was a time she'd read me a story and I'd become concerned that the lovers wouldn't end up together. Perhaps Rapunzel, when the witch throws the prince from the tower, blinding him. I'd always hated and loved that story. I remembered crying over it...

But the point was a good one, whether I'd imagined it or remembered it. Things might seem hopeless now, but it doesn't mean the story is over.

The door to the cabin slammed open, banging against the wall and startling me so that I sat up, my heart pounding.

"Sorry," Zack said, carrying in a tray. "Were you asleep? I couldn't knock with this thing." He set the tray down at the end of the cot. "It's not much, just beef and gravy, but it's not terrible. Doesn't have weevils in, at least."

I scrunched my nose at his disclaimer, but the gravy smelled good and I hadn't eaten in a while. I pulled the plate towards me.

"Thank you. Does it... does it often have weevils?"

Zack shrugged and pulled a chair over, sitting beside the bed. "In the hard tack, yeah. It's horrible."

I shuddered. The crew of the Kelpie took turns cooking, and we often had fresh food, and if it wasn't fresh, then it was interestingly spiced. Tate didn't allow food to go bad on the ship. I had forgotten the Navy had no such stipulations. I started to eat.

"So, have you uh, had a chance to think about what I said?" Zack asked, not looking at me, and speaking softly, as if embarrassed.

"I've had nothing but time to think," I snapped. Then I regretted my tone, because it wasn't Zack's fault I was shut up in here with no one to talk to. "Sorry. Yes, I've considered it, and I'd like to cooperate with you. Lord knows I need some help."

"Right," Zack licked his lips and swallowed. "Well, the thing is, when we was down in the brig, I could see how you were with those two men. And I saw how they were with you, and... I believe you. I don't think you was kidnapped." He sighed his breath out and gazed at me, his eyes wide.

Something eased in my chest, some taut string loosened and I felt my shoulders relax. I swallowed the mouthful I'd been chewing and smiled tentatively. "Really?"

"Yes, you said I love you to them and they believed it, didn't even blink, and I reckon... I reckon what you said was true, that you ran away. And now your lovers are locked up and you'd do anything to save them."

I inhaled, raised my eyebrows. "Well, yes. That's. That's very astute of you."

Zack met my eyes and a look of fear crossed his face. "And I reckon that if you're a queer and you have more than one lover, then you probably wouldn't judge me for what I am."

There's the link, the secret. Zack's queer too, perhaps?

"I won't judge you," I said, quickly. I set the empty plate aside and shuffled a little closer to him. "Whatever it is, you can tell me, Zack."

"I..." Zack hesitated, looked back at the door, as if to ensure it wasn't suddenly open, then leaned in to whisper to me. "I wasn't born a boy."

"Oh," I said. I smiled. "That's all right. I've learned a lot of things about gender since I joined the Kelpie, and the main thing I've learned is that it actually doesn't matter."

Zack blinked at me, eyes wide. His mouth dropped open. "It... what?" His face had gone quite pale so I reached for his hand and squeezed it.

"Well, I don't know if you saw the Quartermaster," I said. "But she's a woman and she has a beard. Her name is Sagorika, you could... I don't know if you're allowed onto the Kelpie, but you could go and see her and talk to her, maybe. I don't know."

"I don't think I'm allowed," Zack said, but his eyebrows drew together.

"And one of my other lovers, they don't have a gender at all, they're both and neither. And they're absolutely wonderful," I said.

"*One* of your *other* lovers? Isn't two enough?" Zack exclaimed and then clapped his hand over his mouth. "Sorry," he said, muffled. "I didn't mean to judge you."

"It's all right," I said, laughing a little. "I know it's nothing like what polite society would accept. But on the Kelpie, things are different." I thought back to my first day, when I'd first met Sagorika and been surprised. What had she said to me then? "It's a place where you can be yourself, whatever that might be. No one will judge you for it."

"It sounds too good to be true," Zack snatched his hand away from mine and huffed.

I tried not to feel hurt at this. I knew, better than anyone, perhaps, how unbelievable it sounded. But it did hurt a little, all the same, to not be trusted.

"I know it does," I said. "It's a lot to take in. But..." I trailed off as the semblance of a plan started to form in my head. I swallowed and continued talking to get it out of my head and into Zack's. "Listen, life here on the Trinity Royal can't be easy for you. How do you change clothes? Relieve yourself? Do you lower your voice when you speak?"

"All the time," Zack said and rolled his eyes. "And yeah it's horrid, I can't always remember and I'm terrified someone will notice."

"And if they found out, what would they do?"

"I'd be dropped at the first port, dishonourable discharge. Or maybe they'd scrub my record entirely." He answered so fast I knew it wasn't a hypothetical, spur of the moment response. He had considered this at length. Probably often. I could just imagine him sleepless in his hammock, full of fear at being found out.

"What if you..." I cleared my throat, afraid of how he'd take this. "What if you helped me to get Tate and Ezra out of there, and back to the Kelpie? You could join us, leave the Navy and sail with people who'd accept you, knowing the truth?"

Zack's face flushed red and his eyes widened before he shook his head. "No, I couldn't. I'm here to make my fortune."

"Oh," I said. I couldn't hide my disappointment, and something told me I shouldn't - that maybe seeing my misery a little more would help my cause.

Zack watched me and then looked away.

"I'd... I'd have to think about that. I don't think I could. But. But maybe I can help with the first part of the plan, anyway," he said.

My heart soared, that was more than I could reasonably have hoped for.

"You can? Thank you, that would be wonderful. Really, I'm so alone here and I can't stand the thought of either of them being led to the gallows."

Zack shuddered a little and nodded. "I want to help, I do. I just need to... give me tonight and I'll see what I can do to help."

I reached for his hand again and he let me take it, so I clasped it in both of mine.

"Thank you, really, any amount of help you can give will make a world of difference. Thank you, Zack."

Zack nodded and the corner of his mouth twitched, pulling up into a tiny smile.

"I'll be back in the morning with your breakfast, we can talk then."

I let go of his hand as he stood. He took the dinner tray and went to the door. He paused there, and turned back, gave me an inscrutable look and then was gone.

Alone again.

What am I supposed to do all night?

CHAPTER FIVE - IN WHICH GIDEON'S LUCK TURNS

I circled the room once and sat back down, sighing. I couldn't stand it. The room was too small and I was too alone.

The door wasn't locked.

I got up and left the room, feeling that if I didn't, I'd surely explode from loneliness or boredom or both.

I strode out onto the deck as if I were supposed to be there. Even though I had no shoes and only basic issue clothes on.

Most of the crew had gone below deck to sleep by this time. It was night, and the moon hung above the ship, a bright white crescent. I could see the Kelpie moored close by, so close you could lay a plank between the two ships and walk from one to the other. I supposed they'd been switching watches back and forth. I wondered if anyone was sleeping in my cabin.

It was so close. Freedom itself, so close.

But so many obstacles in my way.

I had to protect my lovers, I knew then I would do absolutely anything to save them from our current predicament and the imminent dangers.

Someone approached me on the deck, their boot heels rapping on the wood. I didn't bother to turn, I couldn't tear my eyes from the Kelpie. It was so close I could almost touch it and I didn't care which member of the Royal Fleet it was.

"Master Keene," a voice said. I didn't recognise it, but it was full sounding, the vowels well rounded and refined.

I inhaled and turned then. A quick look at his uniform and I saw he was a Commander. I guessed his age to be mid to late twenties. He had large dark eyes and long eyelashes and his frame was slim.

"Commander... ?" I asked, although I could barely bring myself to care about his answer.

"Carrol," he said. "You shouldn't be up on deck."

"Shouldn't I?" I raised an eyebrow at him. I felt like there was little I had left to lose, and if this man wanted to exert his power over me then it wouldn't matter. He had no official power over me, after all.

My emotions swirled, desolate and giddy at the same time.

"You should be convalescing in your room, in the infirmary, Master Keene."

"I'm not sick," I said. "Nor am I injured. And I was under the impression, Commander Carrol, that I'm not a prisoner on this ship. The Captain said I should stay out of the way of the men, but I don't see any drills being run at this particular time."

"No." Commander Carrol said. "But with the Kelpie so close..." he trailed off and I wondered what he'd been thinking of saying.

I looked back at the Kelpie and frowned, seeing something small and black dart over the deck and up the rigging.

That wasn't... could it be?

I let my eyes follow the line of the mast up. The ships were close, the yardarms a good few feet apart but that was nothing of a jump to a cat...

My heart swelled with hope and happiness.

I couldn't let Commander Carrol notice what I'd seen.

Turning back to him, I cleared my throat and put on a polite smile. "How did you earn your rank, Commander? You seem young to have got so far already."

His stern face softened and he smiled back at me.

"Thank you, hard work I assure you. Although my father's position surely made it easier to do that hard work in the first place."

"I'm sure." I gave a little laugh.

Is he flirting with me? He's certainly not repulsed by my flirting with him. He's not an ugly man. Certainly he's no Tate, Ezra, Ora, or Zeb, I don't care for him the way I love them. But this is as good a way to keep his attention.

Then something happened inside me, a sort of unfurling, maybe, like a flower blooming in my chest. Suddenly, I knew just what to say to get him to like me.

"I'm sure your father is very proud of you, making something of yourself out here," I said. I moved a half step closer to him. "Not just anyone could get to this rank."

It was hard to tell for sure in the moonlight, but I think he blushed at that. He certainly dropped his eyes and fluttered his thick eyelashes before giving me a coy smile.

But of course he did, you're irresistible.

I don't know where this knowledge or this self assurance came from but I liked it. Having even a tiny bit of power here was refreshing.

"You're too kind, Master Keene."

Master... imagine him on his knees, looking up at me, a collar around his neck, naked and begging me to bind him and fuck him. That's real power.

I could just push and maybe he'd...

Wait, why was I imagining that? I didn't want this man. But I knew - on some strange base level - that I could have him if I tried.

This voice in my head was different to any I'd heard before. Maybe it was my magic?

I could see how receptive Carrol was to my flirting and I knew without a doubt that I could continue to push this. I could use my appeal as a weapon and gain power over him...

I pulled back and swallowed, breaking eye contact. I didn't want that power. But it might be useful for a moment. I forced myself to look at him again and gave a smile I didn't feel at all.

"You're in a fine position on this ship," I started, trying to make my voice into something of a purr. "Perhaps you're privy to the mysterious ways the Captain has of communicating over long distances?"

"Oh, yes," Carrol smiled, pleased with himself. "A network of witches, who'd have imagined such a thing? I could hardly believe it when he showed me the box."

"Fancy that," I said, faintly.

Right, the box on Thornton's desk, I knew there was something odd about it. Perhaps that was the source of the power, some amulet or trinket that allowed - what? Magic communication with a witch?

But which witch?

I turned away, I had the information I needed from him now.

"It uh, it must be time to turn in," I said and feigned a yawn. "Goodnight, Commander."

"Indeed, rest well," he said.

I walked briskly back down to my cabin, my heart racing with the horror of what I'd felt, how I could have pushed at the Commander and what? Had him in my cabin on his knees? Had him take me to his cabin and we'd enjoy each other?

Why had that impulse come to me when I didn't want it? Didn't want him?

What was this magic inside me? What was the purpose of such a power?

Whatever it was, I didn't like it.

I went into the infirmary and sat on my bed, then I dropped

my head into my hands and tried to calm the powerful whirlpool of emotions swirling within me.

I don't know how long I sat in that position with the same questions swirling through my head, but eventually I became aware of a familiar sound.

Something was scratching at my door.

All my confusion and fear evaporated as I leapt to my feet and opened the door. A black cat ran into the room, meowing. He ran past me and jumped on the bed. I closed the door and turned back to him.

"Zeb? Is that you?"

The cat shuddered and arched his back, then in an instant, he was Zeb the man. Utterly naked.

"Who else?" Zeb asked, grinning toothily.

I threw myself into his arms and felt a wave of relief wash through me. He wrapped his arms around me and chuckled, and I found myself giggling as well. I was so happy.

"I'm so glad you're here, how did you... how did you learn how to change forms?"

"Well," Zeb said, his mouth was in my hair and his voice came out muffled. "I did it by accident when we lost, and that was good because it meant they couldn't lock me in the cage with the others, and I could hide from them around the ship.

Then I found Ora the night before last and they showed me how to do it."

I sat up a little to look at him properly, take stock of him.

He had no bruises that I could see, no cuts or scrapes, and he seemed happy enough.

"So, Ora's all right, too? That's good to know, they said the ocean was dangerous at the moment."

Zeb nodded. "They've stayed close to the ships, out of sight as much as possible. They're so worried about you, so I suggested I come over to check up on you."

My heart tugged painfully and I shook my head.

"You can tell them I'm all right, and Ezra and Tate are all right too, but they're locked in the brig."

"I can pick the locks," Zeb said. He half sat up and I had to grab onto his shoulders to stop being tipped off his lap. "We can get back to the ship, all of us together."

"Wait, we have to plan more than that. There's too many men, and there are guards. There's always people on watch and they won't just let us walk away with their prisoners."

"We can kill them."

"No, Zeb, we can't just kill everyone," I said, quickly. He rubbed his cheek against mine.

"I don't see why not," he wheedled. I sighed, but I couldn't resist pushing my cheek against his in return.

"Because, if we kill a whole lot of Naval sailors then they'll raise the bounty on all of us, and that will mean a whole lot more of these ships will be hunting us down. We have to handle this as intelligently as we can."

Zeb rubbed his cheek on the other side of my face. Marking me like he was still in cat form, I supposed.

"Love you," Zeb said, and kissed me hard. I melted into his bare chest. Relief and happiness flooded my body and I felt like the world was coming right again, in some small way.

"I love you," I said.

I startled as the door to the infirmary slammed against the wall again. I tried to sit up but Zeb's arms were tight around me. Zack stood in the doorway, his eyes wide and mouth hanging open.

"Oh, what? I don't... who is this? Oh, he's naked, I'll just..." Zack half turned and I shook my head.

"Zack, no it's all right, come back. Zeb, let go of me," I said. I pulled against Zeb's hold and he let go. "Just, uh, come in and shut the door, please."

Zack stared at Zeb and then did as I asked, closing the door and focusing their gaze on me instead.

"I don't understand," Zack said, softly. "Who is this?"

"This is Zeb, he's a cat some of the time," I said. "And uh, he's one of my lovers, obviously."

Zack's jaw worked, so I gave them some time to think. I turned to pull the blanket over Zeb and shook my head at his grin.

"Cover yourself up so that Zack doesn't get more frightened, please."

"Wait, did you say that he's a cat?" Zack asked.

I turned to Zack, and reached for his hand. "Listen, I don't want to get into all of that right this second. Zeb sneaked on board and had some news for me. Are you still willing to help me break Captain Tate and Ezra out of the brig? I know you said that you needed tonight to think it through..."

Zack shook his head and took a breath before speaking. "I didn't need time. I want to do the right thing, and everything about them being taken to the gallows feels wrong to me. I want to help you Master Keene."

"Call me Gideon, please," I said. But my chest flooded with warmth and I felt myself positively beaming at him. "Thank you, with Zeb's help it should be easier than I thought."

"We'll wait until the fourth bell of the Middle watch," Zack said.

That put it at roughly two in the morning.

"That makes sense," I said. "Most of the people on board will be asleep."

"I don't know if I can sneak a key to the cell, though," Zack said.

"Zeb can pick the lock," I said.

Zeb sat up and put his arm around my shoulders. The blanket had fallen away again. I rolled my eyes and pulled it over his lap.

"How much fighting can we expect?" he asked.

Zack shrugged, his eyes very carefully directed up and past our heads, his cheeks pink.

"If everyone's asleep maybe not much… but there's Naval officers on the pirate ship."

"Ora can deal with them, I think," I said, although I hated suggesting it, this was a desperate time. We had to get away and that was the most important thing. "Can you ask them to, Zeb? Disable the Naval crew on the ship?"

Zeb nodded. "I could help, as well."

"If the alarm is raised the Trinity will fire," Zack said. "Maybe with the cannons…"

"I don't think I can wander around on deck and mess with the workings of the cannons," I said, slowly. I eyed Zack.

Zack looked away and shook his head. "No, I can't… if this doesn't work I can't be seen to have been helping you."

"Oh, yes, that makes a lot of sense, I don't want you to get into trouble if things go badly." I swallowed, but I refused to entertain the thought that this plan wouldn't work.

"I can do it," Zeb said. "I'll shift back and pee on all the powder."

"Zeb, some of that powder will be in barrels," I said. "Look for the wicks, and the lashings fastening the cannons down and for goodness sake, don't let anyone see you." I kissed him, afraid all over again.

"I shouldn't… I can't hear this," Zack said. "I'll go, and uh, leave the two of you to… it…" he blushed dark red and went to the door.

"Wait, one more thing, Zack. Is there any chance you can find the uh, the leather collar and cuffs I was wearing when I was… rescued? They have sentimental value to me."

Zack's blush actually deepened. "I'll see what I can do, I think I know where they were put…" And he fled.

Oh God, I hoped that wasn't what was in the box in Thornton's cabin.

"I'll see you later on though?" I asked, as the door shut behind him.

"So, we have a bit of time, then," Zeb said, and rubbed his cheek against mine. His hand slipped down my chest and down, but I caught his wrist and pulled it back.

"Zeb, no. You have jobs to do, we need to get this plan started and it can't go wrong, it just can't. We have to get Ezra and Tate out of the brig but first you need to go talk to Ora. And do something about the cannons, got it?"

"Urgh, fine," Zeb pulled his hand back and shifted into cat form. I tried to pet his head and he growled angrily and jumped off the bed. I opened the cabin door for him and he streaked off into the night.

There was still so much of the cat in him, it was kind of incredible. I forgot some of the time, and then I'd be reminded all over again.

More than anything, I wanted to go down to the brig and reassure Ezra and Tate, but I couldn't risk doing anything involving leaving the infirmary. The less anyone suspected me the better it would be in the long run.

Instead, I lay down on the bed and tried to rest, so I'd be ready to go when Zack returned.

Although I had thought sleep impossible, I fell into a fitful slumber, full of anxious dreams of being caught, watching Tate, Ezra or both hang, or being led to the gallows myself.

The hours ticked by far too slowly.

CHAPTER SIX - IN WHICH AN ESCAPE IS MADE

Finally, I was roused by the scratching on the door, indicating Zeb's return. I hurried to open the door and allow him in, closing the door quickly behind me.

"Zeb, how'd it go?

Zeb blinked at me and refused to change back into human form - no doubt so he could continue sulking.

I scratched behind his ears until he purred and explained to him that once we were all safe back on the Grey Kelpie he could have his way with me all he liked, provided he was back in human form for it. And finally he rolled onto his side and let me rub his belly and we both felt a lot better, I think.

I heard the bells for the Middle Watch, and then the first, second and third. The ship seemed to be utterly silent around us aside from the creaking of the hull and the lap of waves, and I became nervous that Zack wouldn't do as he said he would.

If Zack didn't come to help out, Zeb and I would creep down to the brig ourselves...

I feared without Zack's help we'd be caught, that the worst would come to pass.

Silently, I sent a prayer up to my mother.

Please, Mother, you were always kind to me, you've always steered me well. Please let this work. Please let me save the men I love and allow us to live together again.

And, if you can, please soothe Father somehow. Cool his temper and let him forget me.

The fourth bell of the watch rang and almost the same instant there was the faintest of taps on the door.

I stood up off the bed and Zeb jumped down, purring. I opened the door to Zack, whose eyes were wide and who looked even paler in the light of the lantern he held. He clutched a drawstring bag that he shoved towards me. I took it gratefully.

"Your...effects..."

"Thank you." I slipped the cord over my head and let the bag hang under my shirt, against my chest.

"Ready?" He whispered. I nodded, it wasn't like I had anything to bring from the room. He glanced down at Zeb, who wound around his legs purring and practically smiling up at him.

"Zeb, calm down," I hissed.

"That's Zeb." Zack's voice was utterly toneless.

"You actually do get used to it," I whispered. "Now, please, can we go to the brig now?"

"Yes, I have some keys, I don't think I can get the cell door open but it should unlock the chains." Zack turned and led the way back through the belly of the ship and I followed close behind.

We went into the brig without being challenged which, strangely, just put me on edge even more. As if we had come this far easily, just so that everything would go wrong now.

Tate was snoring but Ezra sat up as we walked in. He shielded his eyes from the light of the lantern.

"What's all this?" He asked.

Tate stirred and sat up slowly and my heart thumped sadly along with the sound of the jingling chains.

"Zeb, this is the lock," I hissed, and tapped the padlock on the cage door. Without warning Zeb shifted back to human form and unpicked the lock with one large claw. Zack looked away from his nakedness and cleared his throat.

"We're rescuing you," I said, moving to the bars to look at the two of them. "This is Zack, he's going to help." I almost said 'he's like us', but I didn't think Zack would appreciate it if I did.

Not the time, and not my secret to tell.

Instead, I watched as Zeb fiddled with the lock. The seconds stretched out and I shifted my weight between my feet, hoping that we would not be disturbed.

There was a clink and Zeb pulled the opened padlock off the door. He swung the door open and beamed at me in the dim lamplight.

Zack handed me the keys and nodded for me to go in. For a moment, I doubted him, and wondered if this was some sort of trap.

He must've seen the fear in my eyes, or the uncertainty.

"Go on, they won't hurt you, they might hurt me," Zack said. "I'll keep watch."

He moved to the door and I went inside the cell, pausing only to kiss Zeb's cheek as I passed.

I sorted through the bundle of half a dozen keys until I found the one that looked about the right size for the metal shackles on Tate's wrists.

"Hello, Gid," he said, softly - his voice was still rough from sleep, which was a state that I knew well by now. It filled me with a warmth I hadn't felt in days.

I stole a kiss from his lips and then set to work, using the key to open the shackles.

"Aaah," Tate said, he rubbed his wrists, stood up and stretched his arms out in front of him as far as they'd go. I imagined he'd like to stretch them up but his head was already brushing the ceiling of the brig. "That feels better."

I moved to Ezra and tried the same key, but it did nothing.

My heart pounded, and my fingers fumbled, almost dropping the keys.

"Calm, pet," Ezra murmured. I took a breath, went back to checking the keys. I found another key of a similar size, and breathed a sigh of relief as the lock clicked open.

Ezra leaned in to kiss me as I pulled the chains off his hands. "Good work, pet, I knew you'd come through for us."

I felt my cheeks flush, but again I refused to be distracted. "Come on, we have to get you out of here."

Tate had already left the cell and was bent, scratching an again-cat Zeb behind the ears. I went to give Zack the keys back, he stuffed them into a pocket in his jacket.

"All ready," Zack said.

He led the way up onto deck, and I was impressed at how silent the four of us - five counting Zeb, which I didn't since he had the soft paddy paws of his cat form - could be. Tate might've been almost seven feet tall but his sneaking didn't expose any of his size.

When we got to the deck, Zack held a hand up and we all froze. He looked around and spotted the two on watch. One of them was leaning against the side of the ship - most of the way asleep, I'd wager, and the other was looking the other way.

"I'll go and distract them, if they stir," Zack said. "You can take the way over Zeb's been using."

"Which way is that?" Tate looked at the Grey Kelpie, anchored alongside the Trinity Royal, so close and also too far away to reach. There were no planks or ladders between the two decks, and I had no idea how we would cross to it.

Zeb mewed softly and led us to the foremast, shifted to human form and quickly and elegantly scaled it, went onto the yardarm and started walking towards the place where the yardarm almost reached that of the Grey Kelpie's mainmast.

"Right, looks easy enough," Tate said. He rubbed his hands together and moved closer to the mast.

My heart started racing and my breath hitched. "What? No, I can't do that. I'll - I'll go over the deck, climb over that way. I'll put down a plank or something." I cast around, looking for the gangplank and seeing nothing. My breath came faster like I had been running.

"Zeb thinks you can cross this way. A plank would alert the watch," Ezra murmured. Honestly, it was a miracle they hadn't already noticed us, I thought.

Tate raised his eyebrows at me. Zack had extinguished his lantern but the moon and the stars gave us enough light to see by. I could see that he needed to shave and tidy up his dashing moustache and goatee.

"No, I can't. You don't understand, I can't do that," I hissed, desperate now, my voice threatening to get louder. I swallowed and rasped. "I'll fall. I'll freeze up there, I'm... I'm absolutely terrified of heights."

Ezra groaned softly. "Yes, I remember you saying now..."

"What if I carried you?" Tate said.

I eyed his huge shoulders and licked my lips. "You couldn't climb like that," I said. "You'd drop me, that would be even worse."

Zeb was already jumping from the Trinity and catching himself on the yardarm of the Kelpie.

"There's no other way," Ezra said. "Either you do it, or we leave you behind, and believe me, we *don't* want to do that."

My heart thundered now, and I could feel sweat slicking my palms and dripping down my back.

"I... I can try," I said, faintly. The words seemed far away even to my own ears.

"You go first, Ezra, and I'll follow Gideon," Tate said.

Ezra nodded and scaled the mast almost as fluidly as Zeb

had, but with his white shirt, he was a lot more obvious. I glanced back at the men on watch and Zack, hiding partially behind another mast between us and the watch.

Some part of me hoped they'd look over and call out so I wouldn't have to follow him.

I moved closer to the mast and put the palm of my hand on it.

That time, when I was meant to be securing the rigging - stuck at the top of the mast as a storm rolled in. The fear, the inability to do anything to save myself for fear of falling to my death.

"Maybe you should go first, Tate," I said.

"Come on, I'll boost you up." Before I could say anything, his hands were on my waist and he was lifting me upwards. I scrabbled my fingers on the mast, trying to find purchase.

"No, I can't," I said, louder this time. I couldn't control the volume of my voice, my chest tightened so far I could hardly breathe.

I can't breathe. My heart is going to stop. I'm going to die and I haven't even got up the mast yet.

"Who's there?" a voice called through the night. Tate tried to push me further up the mast.

"Tate, stop! Let me down!" I cried. He let me down to the deck where I clutched my hand to my chest, trying to soothe the pain there.

"It's just me," Zack said. "Ensign Zacharias!"

"What's going on at the mast?"

"The watch," Tate hissed. "They've seen us."

"The prisoners! The prisoners have escaped!" The watchman shouted. "Raise the alarm!"

"Quick," Zack said, hurrying to the side of the ship. "Take a lifeboat. It's the only way, I'll try and hold them off."

I couldn't move, my heart was thundering in my head. Everything was going wrong. I had no idea what to do.

Tate yanked me by the arm and hauled me to the lifeboats, where Zack was pulling the dinghy up and over the side of the boat on the ropes. Tate hurried to help him.

Behind us, the alarm bell sounded, startling me a little into action.

I had to help. This was *my* rescue and I had to make it work.

I looked up to see Ezra swinging on a rope between the ships' yardarms. He was safe, more or less, although my mouth went dry seeing him so high up.

Tate and Zack lowered the lifeboat to the water as fast as it would go, but there were shouts behind us and that meant the night watchmen were approaching with swords drawn.

I didn't have a weapon - a weapon would've been useful.

The men of the Watch got closer. I cast around for something to grab, but the ship was tidy and well organised, there was nothing just lying around.

"Is that the boy we rescued from the pirate ship?"

"Master Keene, what are you doing?"

"Nothing, just... a midnight stroll on the deck," I bluffed, madly hoping they somehow haven't seen what Tate and Zack were doing.

"Hands in the air, all three of you," one of them said, pulling out a gun.

I swallowed and put my hands in the air, eyeing the gun.

This wasn't going well.

I heard the splash of the lifeboat hitting the water, but Tate and Zack were still on deck. Footsteps rattled from below deck, the rest of the crew of the Trinity Royal. They were all going to be here in a moment.

We had to get off the ship.

But they had guns on us, a lot of people wanting to stop us from leaving.

Then, I saw a shadow pull themselves up from the side of

the ship, glistening wet in the moonlight. They were right behind the two men on watch, who hadn't noticed them yet.

"Please, you don't understand," I said, loudly, trying to make sure the watch kept their eyes on me. "It's not what it looks like, honestly, I'm all right. I was just taking a walk, I wanted to see the moon…"

God, why do I have to be such a poor liar?

"Stop talking!" One of the men on watch said.

Then Ora's hand was around his neck, pulling him. His gun fired, and I flinched. But the barrel of his gun was aimed safely up into the air instead of at me, as his body bent backwards.

The other watchman turned to try and fight but Ora had already discarded the first man's body and leapt to meet him, mouth wide and teeth bared. I turned away, hurrying to the side of the ship where Tate was now scrambling overboard, reaching a hand out to me to join him.

"Gideon, quick!"

Zack helped me over the side, lifting me by the elbow. "Go, now, it's your chance," he said.

"Come with us, Zack," I hissed. I gripped his arm and tugged. "Please, you could be happy with us, you could be yourself and no one would care…"

"I think you'd better come," Tate said, more serious than my urgent begging. "They've seen you with us, and it'd be hard to explain away."

"I… yes, yes, all right," Zack said.

More crew appeared on deck. Zack dove over the side of the ship into the water and Tate hauled him into the rowboat beside him.

I started to row.

The adrenaline surging through my body added strength to my arms, although I was still shaking from my attempt at climbing the rigging.

Faces appeared on over the side of the boat as we made our

short way to the Kelpie. There was a splash as Ora dove into the water from the Royal and soon appeared beside the lifeboat.

Turning, I looked up at the Kelpie and saw Ezra lowering the rope ladder down for us. His eyes met mine and I swallowed hard, reassured to see him where he should be, back on board our ship.

Tate turned to the people watching from the Trinity Royal and shouted at the top of his voice.

"I'm taking Ensign Zack and Gideon Keene as hostages! If you fire upon us or pursue the Kelpie, I'll execute them both!" His voice boomed, silencing the cries from the Trinity.

The men at the edge of the ship murmured, and I heard the loud, bell-like voice of Captain Thornton ring out.

"Hold fire!"

The lifeboat reached the Kelpie and I gestured for Zack to climb up first, which he did quickly and without hesitation.

"You go next Gideon, and try to look afraid of Ezra when you get to the top," Tate murmured. Then he grabbed my arm and hauled me towards the ladder as if it wasn't my main goal and all I wanted.

It wasn't at all hard to feign fear as I scaled the ladder, my stomach turned over and over from dread - Captain Thornton had ordered his men not to fire, but they may still fire upon the Kelpie as we attempted to sail off.

My arms shook as I gripped the ropes of the ladder. I tried to convince myself that this was different from climbing up the mast. The bulk of the ship was right there, and although the ladder swung alarmingly, I knew Tate was behind me, ready to catch me if I fell, and I was climbing towards Ezra and safety.

I trusted Tate and Ezra, I knew they wouldn't leave me behind or let me fall to my death.

I forced myself through it, gritting my teeth hard.

Zeb hadn't said if he'd disabled the cannons or not, and he was in such a contrary mood there was no way of knowing. At any point, the Trinity could fire upon us, although I did believe Thornton would wait until I was obviously safe.

As I reached the top of the ladder, Ezra grabbed hold of my arm and yanked me onto the ship, so hard I fell and cried out as my shoulder hit the deck.

Well, at least they'll believe I'm being kidnapped now, I suppose, I thought, somewhat giddy, relieved the climb was over and I was back home.

At the helm of the Kelpie, I saw Sagorika crouching, waiting until everyone was on board. James and Anton were also on deck, crouched beside the winch for the anchor and slowly turning it.

Tate climbed aboard and called for the anchor to be pulled up. Anton and James leapt to their feet and turned the winch quickly. Ora climbed up the rope ladder and pulled it up behind them. From the shadows the rest of the Kelpie's crew appeared and unfurled the main sails.

My heart soared.

Had the plan worked? Were we actually going to get away?

I got to my feet and Ezra made a show of grabbing my arm and pushing it up behind my back - which was, for us, practically foreplay - and Tate took hold of the back of Zack's shirt.

"You're not to follow us!" Tate shouted again.

The deck rocked and the Grey Kelpie started to move. I pressed myself back against Ezra to let him know how happy I was without giving anything away. I tried to look as frightened as possible, which, again, wasn't difficult given the way my heart was racing and my limbs trembled.

"No, let me go!" Zack said, his voice pitched loudly like an actor's on stage.

On the Trinity the men were moving, swarming around the cannons and readying them. I bit my lower lip.

Erza hauled me back towards Tate's cabin and Tate did the same with Zack.

"Get down, if they mean to fire we could be in trouble," Tate hissed.

Ora opened the door to the cabin and we were pushed inside.

"Maybe not!" I whispered back. "Find Zeb, ask what he did."

Tate winked at me, pushed Ora inside, too, and slammed the door of the cabin.

"Well, that was jolly exciting wasn't it?" Zack said. He turned to Ora. "You killed those men with your mouth, didn't you? Absolutely *terrific*, that was."

"Ora," I ignored Zack for the time being, and threw myself into their arms. "It's so good to see you."

Ora stumbled backwards, their arms going around me and squeezing me tight, laughing a little at my enthusiasm.

Something inside me that had been jangling and afraid settled into its rightful place. I kissed Ora on the mouth and felt a little more like myself, a little more whole.

Ora returned the kiss and moaned softly, and I was trying to push them up against the wall when Zack coughed loudly and I remembered we weren't alone. I pulled back from Ora, although they left their arm around my waist.

"Sorry, right. Ora this is Zack, Zack this is Ora, they're merfolk and don't have a gender, I think I mentioned them before to you."

Zack waved a hand and smiled, although there was nervousness in the smile.

"Hello Ora, it's very uh, nice to meet you." He was looking up at the ceiling and not at us. For a moment I was confounded by his behaviour, and then realised I could feel a lot more of Ora than I should have been able to.

"Oh, uh, Ora, where's your skirt?"

Ora sighed and picked up the nearest piece of clothing and

pulled it on, covering themselves. "You humans are just so strange about your bodies," they said.

Outside the cabin door, I heard Tate and the others laughing.

"That's a good sign," I said. "Isn't it?"

Ora pushed the door open a crack and peeked outside. "What's happening?"

"They can't fire on us," Tate said. "Looks like Zeb came through."

I sighed, feeling the tension leak out of my body, my shoulders relaxing. Zack went to the door to look out as well, but I grabbed his hand and pulled him back.

"Let's just wait until we're definitely out of sight," I said, when he looked back at me. "Make sure the deception that we're hostages holds some water."

"Right, of course."

Ora closed the door again and smiled easily at the both of us, then raised an eyebrow at me. "Is Zack going to join us and be another lover?"

"Oh," I said, glancing at Zack. "I don't *think* so, I didn't assume -"

Zack shook his head very fast. "No, that's not. Not for me, thank you. I don't want... I've never been attracted to men, particularly. I mean -" He looked at Ora and bit his lip. "Sorry, I know you're not a man, but. I've always found women to be the most attractive, and if I was to go for a man, maybe it would be you, Gideon, but no. No. I don't think I could be so all right with all the sharing." He huffed out his breath and smiled sheepishly.

"It's fine, really," I said. "You don't have to explain. We'll find you a hammock down below, or, oh, you could use my old cabin? You'll... you'll be able to hear anything that happens in here though, which... maybe you wouldn't want to." I swallowed. "Well, we'll work something out. If you want privacy the cabin's there."

Zack laughed. "Privacy? I'd hardly imagined... I didn't think it'd be possible."

"You're gonna have to adjust to a lot of what you thought was impossible," I said.

The three of us settled down to wait for the all-clear.

CHAPTER SEVEN - IN WHICH THE HAREM REUNITES

The door to the cabin slammed open and Tate grinned down at me.

"Ensign Zack, if you'd excuse us? Go talk to Sagorika, she's at the helm, she'll find someplace for you to sleep and get new clothes."

"Right, yes, Captain, right away," Zack said, and rushed out of the room. He crashed into Ezra who was attempting to enter the room. "*Oh God*, The Shearwater pirate! I'm so sorry. Please don't hurt me." Zack ducked under Ezra's arm and ran up the deck.

"Don't call me that," Ezra grumbled and came into the room, walking straight over to me and wrapping me in his arms. "I thought you were following me up the mast, that you were right behind me, if I'd realised... I never would have left you behind like that."

"It's fine," I said, although I was somewhat squashed against his chest. "Getting you and Tate clear was the main goal, after all. Oh, and here," I pulled the pouch from around my neck and pressed it into Ezra's hand.

"What's this?" He pulled it open and saw my leather collar and cuffs and shook his head. "How did you?"

"You can thank Zack tomorrow."

Zeb walked in and closed the door behind him, utterly naked.

"Lock the door, will you Zeb?" Tate said. Zeb looked blankly at the door and then at Tate.

"There's no padlock."

"No, use the bolt." Tate reached past Zeb and slid the bolt home.

Ezra let go of me and we all sort of looked at each other for a moment.

"I uh, I'm glad we're all back together," I said, to break the silence, which was threatening to become awkward. "Really, I've missed all of you."

"Gideon, you did such an amazing job!" Tate exclaimed. He crossed the floor to me in two strides and wrapped his arms around me, squeezing me in a hug so enthusiastic he lifted me clear off the ground. I couldn't help but laugh. "I thought we were done for, I thought they'd have kept you from us."

"Zeb did most of the hard stuff," I said. I took advantage of the proximity to kiss Tate. It felt amazing, another piece of my fractured, jigsaw heart falling into place.

Energy rushed through me like heat. A sensation similar to moving closer to a fire and feeling it warming you. I was trembling still, but now it was for a different reason, a far more pleasant one.

"Yes, thank you, Zeb," Ezra said.

"I helped too," Ora said.

I broke the kiss to look over and see Zeb, Ezra and Ora all touching each other. Ora had slipped their skirt off again, they and Zeb were undressing Ezra from the ill-fitting Naval surplus garments.

Tate put me down and I started to undress him, too. Then he gripped me by the shoulders, turned me and pulled my back against his chest. I could feel his hardness pressing against my rear and caught my breath.

"The last time we were all together," Tate murmured in my ear, leaning forward to stroke his hands down my chest. Then he pulled the buttons open on my shirt. "Do you remember what we were doing?"

As if there was any way I could ever forget such an incredible, fantastical experience...

"Yes," I said. "You tied me to the mast and..." My face flushed with the memory, but not from embarrassment or humiliation, but with the heat of the memory. Desire flooded my body like red heat, like fire kindling inside me. I was consumed with *wanting.*

The others turned to look as Tate pulled my shirt off. "Say it out loud, tell us, remind us all what we were doing," Tate urged, louder now, so the others could hear.

"You... Tied me to the mast and all took turns fucking me," I said, a little louder. I was panting already, and my voice sounded hoarse to my ears.

Too much tension, too much longing. Too long I'd missed my gorgeous lovers and needed this - their eyes on me, their hands touching me. The lustful way they looked at me.

Ezra moved to my left-hand side and took my hand, turning it and pulling off the bandage still wrapped around it. There was little damage left from the ropes, but there was a redness there, as if the chafing had happened only hours ago and not several days. With an approving sort of growl he sank his teeth into my wrist right over the mark, sending sparks of pain and hot desire through my arm.

Ora sank to their knees in front of me, using both hands to remove my trousers and pull them swiftly down, closing their mouth over my cock in almost the same movement. Ora's tongue was hot and slick around me and my hips rolled towards their mouth as I sighed with happiness.

Zeb moved to my right-hand side and wrapped an arm around my waist. He pressed against the both of us, and kissed Tate hard on the mouth. I leaned my head back on Tate's shoulder to watch, and then turned to kiss Ezra, who had nipped and kissed his way up my arm.

I shivered, all the sensations getting to be almost overwhelming, but at the same time I was filled with the knowledge that this is what I needed. What I wanted more than anything, yes, but in some way I needed it.

Perhaps it's my magic again? Whatever it is, there's a profound sense of rightness.

Ora bobbed their head on my cock, their tongue roughly caressing my shaft and making it throb. I bit Ezra's tongue by accident and he pulled back.

"Ora, please," I gasped. "I want to last longer…"

Ora sat back and wiped their mouth with the back of their hand, grinning wickedly.

"To the bed," Ezra grunted. Tate let go of me and we all made our way to his huge bed, although Zeb slipped both arms around me and nipped at my ear, making me squirm and moan.

He pushed me down into Ezra's waiting arms so I could continue kissing him. Tate settled alongside me, stroking Ezra's hair back from his face, pressing his chest against my side and Ora was between my legs, licking me open and making me moan into Ezra's mouth.

Zeb settled on the other side, stroking himself as he watched the rest of us. My eyes were mostly closed, but I reached a hand to pull Zeb closer, so I could tease at his nipple with my thumb and forefinger.

The fire inside me had become a steady, hot glow - not threatening to consume me but instead flowing out and into all my lovers. I could feel its heat in my fingertips, and in all the places where I was being touched. I felt powerful, somehow, capable of more than I usually was.

Ezra's hand fisted in my hair and he yanked my head back, gazing at me with hooded eyes.

"Stars, Gideon, what are you doing?" he growled, in wonder.

The tongue that had been probing me withdrew and I whined with the loss of it. Ora shifted, bit the roundness of my rear, making me yelp, and spoke, their voice husky with desire.

"His magic is flowing, I can feel it, increasing the pleasure."

Tate's hand stilled where it was stroking Ezra, his knuckles grazing my belly. "Magic?" he whispered.

"Not bad magic," I said. "Nothing bad, it just..." I closed my eyes and concentrated, trying to understand the power I could feel. The fire had the potential to be dangerous, maybe, but it mostly felt like it was warming us, connecting us in some way. I felt part of the universe, a sense of incredible belonging and being exactly where I was supposed to be.

"It's joining us together," I said finally. "I trust it, it feels so good, so right. Maybe it's just so powerful because I missed you, all of you, so, so much."

Tate's hand shifted and closed around my cock as well as Ezra's, stroking us together. Behind me Ora's fingers, slick with oil stretched me open with a delightful sting.

It has been too long. I wish I never had to be stretched, that I was constantly in use like this, that I could serve and be serviced by all of my lovers constantly.

The thought was a new one, and I wasn't entirely sure it was mine so much as it was my magic's, but I wasn't concerned about it. I had been truthful when I said I trusted my magic. I wanted very much to understand it better, but I was confident that it wasn't hurting anyone.

"Fuck, is he ready yet, Ora?" Ezra groaned.

"Yes I am," I said. I bucked my hips impatiently.

Ora gripped my hips and lifted me so I could shift my knees forward, pulling myself free of Ezra's hands so I could sink down on him. I knocked Zeb's hand away from himself and took over stroking him. Tate still had his hand around my cock, but I still wanted Ora's touch in some way as well.

I twisted, trying to see Ora, to pull them close to me.

"It's all right, love," Ora said, shifting closer. "I'm right here."

My attention was torn between all the sensations around me. I rocked my hips, embedding Ezra deep inside me until I gasped, hearing his moan in response.

I stoked Zeb with one hand, groaning as he pushed up into it, and Tate leaned between Ezra and me to kiss Zeb hard.

Behind me, Ora moved, pressing their chest to my back, one hand joining Tate's on my cock and the familiar push of their cock against my rear.

If only more than one of them could fuck me at once. Is that possible?

The voice of my magic again? It was an intoxicating idea but I had no idea if it would work, and probably not now when I was being stretched for the first time in a while.

I rocked my hips faster, working to bring Ezra off so that Ora could fill me as well. Two hands on my cock pumping and my own hands busy with Zeb's and Tate's. It was overwhelming.

The heat of my magic flowed between all of us and I felt myself at the centre like a keystone, the connection that held everything together, locking the group of us into one sensuous, writhing being of joy.

I bucked my hips and came without warning, and this spurred Ezra on - I felt him flood me with his seed and moaned loudly at the sensation.

Gathering my wits about me even as I shuddered with the aftereffects of my orgasm, I lifted so that Ezra could slip out and Ora immediately pushed inside me. I leaned forward, taking Zeb into my mouth as Tate's cock bucked in my hand.

Below me, Ezra groaned, his hands moving over my head and shoulders, Tate's joining him and someone else's hand in my hair. Zeb's cock was thick and full in my mouth and only took a little sucking before he was filling my mouth and yowling more cat-like than human.

Tate's cock twitched in my hand and he came as well, I felt the seed spurt onto my shoulder and groaned, swallowing down what I could of Zeb and licking him clean.

Ora bucked into me twice, one arm tight around my waist and came, their seed mixing with Ezra's and filling me with more light and fire all over again.

Slowly, the group of us came to a stop, panting, moaning with pleasure.

Ezra laughed - a surprising sound - and Tate bit my shoulder, then licked it clean of his own spending.

Ora pulled out and lay down on top of Tate, I rolled off Ezra and found myself wrapped in Zeb's strong arms instead, the lot of us a tangle of limbs.

"Well, fuck," Tate said. "That was a celebration and a half."

"I feel as if I've drunk two bottles of wine," Ezra said, his voice light with laughter.

"The magic," Ora mumbled, pushing their face under Tate's chin and kissing his Adam's apple. "It connected us all."

"You felt that, too?" I asked, surprised. Although Ora was a magician, a magic-user themself, so probably it shouldn't have surprised me.

Zeb rumbled against my back. "Felt it, saw it," he said. "It's like catnip…"

"Need to find a witch," Ora said. "Find out what it means."

Tate met my eyes and I saw something there I never wanted to see again - fear. I cleared my throat.

"Yes, we need to find a witch," I said. "I want to be able to control it."

"Well, Captain's set a course for Nassau," Ezra said. "There's bound to be witches in Nassau." He closed his eyes, apparently already half asleep. I felt weariness dragging at my eyelids, too.

"That's right." Tate said. He half sat up, one arm holding Ora close against his chest and kissed me. "It's going to be all right, whatever happens."

"I never want to be split apart from you like that again," I said. I pressed myself closer to Zeb, who wrapped his arms even tighter around me. Ezra's hand found my hair and he played with it gently.

"Never again," Ora said, their voice muffled against Tate's beard.

And then I let weariness take me and fell into a blissfully restful and dreamless sleep.

In the morning there was no shouts of orders from a Naval officer, there was no cold, lonely bed and no picture of a human skeleton on the wall. Instead, I woke up warm, tangled in the limbs of my lovers. Rapturously happy, I nuzzled Zeb and then Ezra as they were the closest.

Finding Ezra still in bed was another delight, but perhaps one that should just be put down to exhaustion rather than a desire to snuggle.

Whatever the reason, it didn't matter. I was home with the ones I loved and the British Navy was surely leagues behind us.

I stretched and sighed, relishing the way my limbs felt well used and well-rested. My movement disturbed the others through. Ezra shifted onto his side, which nudged Tate who woke up with a start.

He caught me looking at him and smiled, keeping eye contact as he kissed Ora's dark curls and made them hum with happiness.

My heart was full.

Zeb's arms tightened around me and he grumbled. He never liked to wake up in the morning, let alone get up.

I rested my head on his bicep and closed my eyes - there was

no harm in taking a little more time to rest, especially when Tate
- the Captain of the ship - didn't seem at all concerned.

I woke again a while later. Ezra was sitting up, blinking blearily,
and Tate was pulling on fresh clothes, his own clothes instead of
the borrowed Naval issue garments.

Zeb had relaxed his hold on me and was sprawled on his
back, snoring lightly. Ora blinked their eyes open and met my
gaze with a sweet smile.

"Morning, Gideon," Ora murmured. Ezra shifted off the bed
and I reached out to Ora, who threaded our fingers together.

"Good morning," I said.

"Actually it's afternoon now," Tate said. "I'm going to take the
helm and let Sagorika sleep."

I yawned and sat up, unable to stop myself from smiling
foolishly. Ezra rubbed his hand over his face and pulled on the
trousers he'd been wearing, then left the cabin - presumably to
find his own black clothes instead.

Ora sat up, shuffled over and slipped their arms around me. I
leaned against them.

"Do you need help with anything, Tate?" I asked, closing my
eyes and inhaling Ora's familiar scent.

"I don't think so," he said. "Although... laundry probably
needs doing." I could hear the grin in his voice and I cracked
an eye open to see him grinning mischievously. The
bedclothes certainly needed washing after last night, I
supposed.

"Fine," I said. Ora kissed the top of my head, which ignited
some warm sparks inside me.

"I'm going for a swim," Ora said.

"Wait, didn't you say the ocean was too dangerous for you?" I
straightened up and looked Ora in the eyes.

"Not too many merfolk around this area," Ora said,

shrugging. "There's been some... some battles, I guess, but my kind generally prefer it further South."

"Battles?" Zeb asked. "I like battles."

"I don't suppose you'd like the under the ocean ones," I said.

"Battles, and I... my people have made some enemies. The Green Kelp clan is not well looked at," Ora said.

I frowned. "Are you sure it's safe? I don't want you getting caught up in something because of your family. Lord knows my father has caused enough trouble for us, and he's not even merfolk."

Ora nodded. "It'll be fine, love," they kissed my cheek and smiled. "Don't worry so."

Ora stood up and stretched before skipping out the door after Tate.

I turned to Zeb. "You're going to have to move."

"No," Zeb said. He was stretched on the bed, looking utterly comfortable.

"Orders are orders, and I have to change the bedclothes." I tugged at the corner of the sheet and Zeb growled low in his throat.

"No, I'm sleeping!"

"You're not sleeping, you're talking to me," I said. "Now move."

With a lot of grumbling, Zeb rolled off the bed and left the cabin, barely pausing to pull on a pair of trousers. I got dressed as well, luxuriating in my own clothes for the first time in days.

I stripped the bed and carried the linens down below deck to the place the fresh laundry was stored, smiling wide because even though this was a chore, and Zeb had been annoying, I was back home on the Kelpie, and all was right with the world.

Once I'd sorted the bed linens, I made my way to my old cabin, the one I'd been given when I'd first joined the crew of the Grey Kelpie. My heart thumped nervously, as I wasn't sure if the Naval officers would have looted anything out of there. I didn't have too many precious items, just the one thing I was really eager to see. If they'd taken it, I don't know what I would have done, but then, my mother's portrait held no value to anyone but myself.

And there she was, just where I'd left her. I went to pick up the frame and sat on the bed, gazing into her eyes and smiling.

"We have so much to catch up on, Mother," I began. "To start with, I made a new friend, Zack, and I think you'd really like him. He's different, he used to look like a girl but he's a boy, and he joined us because we're open about that sort of thing, and don't care as much as, well, as civilised society."

I took a breath and regaled her with the whole adventure, and how scared I had been and how pleased I was now.

Her eyes were so warm, watching me, and I could almost feel her in the cabin with me, her presence comforting and gently amused. It was like a warm hug.

I took the portrait into Tate's cabin and set it on his desk so she wouldn't be too far away from me in the future.

Then, I went to see the rest of my friends. Sagorika was in her cabin with Zack, and the door stood open so I knocked on it and cleared my throat.

"Uh, excuse me?"

"Gideon, sugar, come on in," Sagorika called out. I went in and found Zack dressed in his white naval shirt and a pair of brown breeches, seemingly quite relaxed and enjoying a cup of tea. Sagorika wore her simple linen shift dress and poured another cup as I walked in. Her hair was loose about her shoulders, and it appeared her beard was freshly shaven. She got up to hug me, and I returned it happily.

"Hi Gideon," Zack said, smiling shyly.

I expected that since now we were on my ship, and not his,

he felt a little shy of me, despite his apparently relaxed demeanour.

I sat down quickly on the edge of Sagorika's bed. "I hope you're settling in all right?"

Sagorika handed me a teacup - quite fine china, I noted - and I thanked her.

"Very well," Zack said. "Sagorika's been kind enough to take me under her wing."

"He's sleeping in here with me," Sagorika said. "But not like *that*, honey. Just as friends, or well. Family, I suppose."

Although it should have seemed strange for dark-skinned Sagorika to refer to Zack, who was pale as milk, as family, I understood. Family didn't have to mean blood after all.

"I'm so pleased," I said. "I hope the whole, uh, ship capture and so on wasn't too horrid?" I cringed at myself and shook my head. "Sorry, of course it was."

Sagorika sighed. "Well, it wasn't pleasant, that's for sure. Crammed in there with all the men. At least they fed us well, although some of those Naval boys were very rude to me."

"I'm sorry," Zack said, quickly.

Looking down, Sagorika smoothed down her skirt and frowned. "I hate to think what might've happened if it had gone on too much longer."

"And people say pirates are the ones to watch out for," I said, sighing.

Sagorika shrugged one shoulder. "Just that this ship isn't like the stories."

There was silence for a moment and I shook my head and cleared my throat. "Anyway, good, I'm glad the two of you are becoming friends."

"I've put him in the ledger," Sagorika said. "Just as regular crew. I'm very much looking forward to seeing what he cooks us for dinner."

Zack wrinkled his nose. "I'm not much of a cook, I'm warning you now. You'll be disappointed."

Sagorika yawned and I sipped the last of my tea, feeling a wave of sympathy for her. "I suppose you were up all night sailing us out of there?"

She nodded. "Uh huh, and I'm about to kick the both of you out so I can get some rest."

"Of course," I set my teacup down, stood up and kissed her cheek. "Thank you for everything, Sagorika."

"Thank you for getting our Captain and First Mate back," she said, clasping my hand.

"I couldn't have done that without Zack's help," I said, turning to him.

"Yes, you could have. I was useless in the end," Zack said, glumly. "If you don't mind Sagorika, I'd like a nap, too. I'm bone weary."

"Stay if you like," she said, and gave me a wink I couldn't interpret. Perhaps for all her 'family' talk, Sagorika did have her eye on Zack? It was hard to say.

I left them to it and wandered out onto the deck. Ezra was at the helm and Tate was inspecting the ship, checking all the lines and cannons.

"Checking the Navy didn't ruin the ship?" I asked him, as I got closer.

"It did. The question is how much. I'm checking the extent of the damage," Tate said. He sighed and dusted his hands on his trousers. "We might have to anchor somewhere closer before we get all the way to Nassau, but we should at least make it to the Bahamas."

I nodded and looked at the horizon behind us, scanning in case there were ships there.

"Not to worry," Tate said, catching the direction of my gaze. He put his arm around me. "Zeb's up in the crow's nest keeping an eye out. Haven't seen anything. I think they really didn't follow us."

"That's good for now, but -" I realised I hadn't shared everything I'd learned on the Trinity Royal with him. "Captain Thornton has something that connects him to a witch. And I uh, I have the feeling that Solomon was the witch he was talking to. Or, Solomon's involved somehow. Carrol said there's a whole network, and given the timing of the ship coming across us..."

Tate sighed and folded his arms, I pouted as he stopped touching me and then caught myself being ridiculous.

"Yes, I admit I had considered that. But I don't understand, I thought Solomon would have wanted to finish me off himself, that ship was taking us to Kingston to be hanged." Tate frowned at the horizon.

I shrugged, uncertain myself, except for one point. "Maybe he would've directed them to sail past the Splintered Isles?"

"Maybe so."

I sighed. "I hated feeling so helpless when they attacked."

"Well," Tate grinned and quirked an eyebrow at me. "You were tied to the mast."

"There was that, yes." My cheeks heated from the memory and I glanced at the mast again before continuing. "Even if I hadn't been. I know I'm out of practice with my sword, and I want to be of more use. Sagorika offered to teach me a little, but she's looking out for Zack and I'd rather he settled in easily. Do you think you could do some, uh, drills with me?"

"Oh, of course," Tate said. "After the days in that blasted cell, I could use some exercise myself. Good idea, Gid."

For the next five days, I settled into a new routine. In the morning I'd wake up with Tate and Zeb - Ezra and Ora having returned to their customary sleeping places - and Tate and I would do sword exercises together on the deck.

Then I'd wash and do whatever needed doing around the ship - not that there was much. Just keeping the ledger up to date and making sure Tate's cabin was clean and tidy. In the afternoon I'd spent time with Ora, or with Ezra, and then after dinner some combination of my lovers would take me to bed. It was a very agreeable routine.

On the sixth day the islands of the Bahamas were sighted. At the shout of land, Tate gathered the crew on the deck and addressed them.

"Since our encounter with the British Navy, we've all been a bit on edge, myself included," Tate said. He'd raised his voice so everyone could hear him but his tone was genial.

There was a rumbling of agreement through the crew. I was standing beside Zack, who had his hands shoved in his pockets and was looking concerned.

"So, we're going to have a bit of a break, bit of shore leave, if you like." He grinned and a few of the crew tittered. "Before we get to Nassau, we're going to anchor at a beach and spend a few days on repairs. You'll each have a couple of shifts working on the ship, and a shift or two fishing, but other than that, just relax and enjoy yourself. We can set up some tents and things on the beach if you fancy sleeping out."

The crew cheered.

Zack's eyes bulged and he leaned in to whisper in my ear. "What? We're just going to be idle?"

I shrugged and nodded. "Seems like, doesn't it sound good?"

"Sounds too good to be true, if you ask me," Zack said, but the concern had gone from his expression and he started to smile.

"Ora, will you scout us out a suitable spot, please?" Tate said, turning to the merfolk. They nodded and promptly stripped off their skirt and jumped overboard.

"I'll never get used to that," Zack said, sighing.

"Never say never," Ezra said, appearing behind me and making us both jump.

"Hello Ezra," I said, smiling and going to put my arms around him for a kiss. Since his capture, he'd been more open to my touching him and giving him affection, and I wanted him to get accustomed to it because I loved it so much. Selfish of me, really.

"How do you feel about some training once we're at anchor?" he asked.

My cock immediately sprang to attention and I pressed myself against Ezra from thigh to chest.

"Training?" Zack asked. I glanced at him.

"Uh, you... you most likely don't want to know the details, Zack," I said. Zack opened his mouth, closed it again and then nodded.

"Right you are, see you later." He turned and left us alone. Ezra chuckled low.

"You like that idea, do you?"

"Yes, uh, yes Master, I do," I said, rocking my hips against his to show him just how much.

Ezra took hold of the back of my neck and kissed me hard, one of those bone-melting kisses that made my knees weak and my cock even harder.

He broke the kiss and grinned at me. "That's a promise for later, you just keep on thinking about it, pet."

I breathed out heavily, struggling to get myself under control as he let go of me.

"So cruel," I breathed, which just made him laugh.

CHAPTER NINE - IN WHICH THE KELPIE ANCHORS IN A SAFE HARBOUR

Ora returned after an hour with news of an uninhabited island with a safe harbour hidden behind a volcanic peninsula. They led the ship in past the coral reef and into the deep, round lagoon.

With the sails down it seemed the ship would be invisible from the ocean sea, and the beach looked beautiful - white sands and coconut palms leading up to a mountain a little way off.

The Kelpie anchored in the lagoon and Tate declared a free afternoon for everyone except for one lookout.

Several of the crew jumped right into the lagoon and swam around, laughing. I waited until one of the longboats was readied and took that onto the beach itself.

I'd been keeping my hair loose around my shoulders, and it felt blissful to have the gentle warm wind blowing through it. There were flowering bushes where the sand gave way to forest, and the scent of the blooms wafted in the breeze - mingling pleasantly with the salt spray.

The sun was hot above, so I stood with my feet in the gentle waves where they washed the sand. Anton and James were swimming in from the ship at a leisurely pace, calling and laughing to each other. I began to wonder if there was an attraction between them, as they often seemed to be together. But possibly they were just friends, and my own apparently insatiable desires were colouring my interpretations of things.

Zeb had come on the longboat with me, but he became distracted when he saw a school of fish in the shallows. He was now standing in water up to his knees, half bent, one hand with long claws held out and ready to pounce, his eyes fixed on the water.

He looked like a Roman statue of a handsome man, one of those with their muscles elegantly carved from marble, their rears round and perfect. The ideal...

He held himself completely still, only his eyeballs moving, and I had no doubt he'd catch a fish soon enough.

Ora was still swimming, I could see them jumping out of the water over near the ship, the scales of their tail catching the sunlight and glinting, sprays of water splashing up when they dove in again, happy as a dolphin.

Sagorika and Zack were still on the ship, preparing some hot food for dinner that night, although they had sworn it wouldn't take too long.

Shem had volunteered for first look out duty, and was installed in the crow's nest with a spyglass.

Tate was on the second longboat, with Ezra, the two of them escorting some bottles of rum and casks of wine for the celebration we would surely have that night. I dug my toes into the wet sand and let a thrill of excitement wash over me.

With alcohol, everyone's inhibitions were loosened, and I looked forward to something new with one, two or all of my lovers.

Ezra looked over and saw me and I swear I felt his gaze on me like a cold splash of water. I remembered his promise to give me some more training.

I had no idea what form the training would take - the last proper session we'd had was in Tortuga, when he'd bound me with leather... it had been delicious.

It was hard to imagine such things as leather paraphernalia on the beach though, so much sand and water... but then Ezra did love it all, I couldn't rule it out. I just had no way to know what to anticipate, aside from it being incredibly fun and fulfilling.

Not knowing added to my excitement, which I'm sure was his aim.

I went to help them unload the bottles and baskets of food they'd brought ashore. We found a shaded spot up the beach to stack the things on a low rock. Then Tate opened one of the wine bottles and swigged directly from the bottle.

I cringed a little, but even my former etiquette master would concede that we couldn't exactly bring fine crystalware onto the beach with us.

"Here you are, Gid." He offered me the bottle, and I resisted the urge to wipe the opening with my shirt sleeve. It may seem unsanitary, I told myself, but I had shared saliva with Tate on many occasions, and more private bodily fluids as well.

"Thank you."

I gamely took the bottle and drank directly from the neck of it, feeling the alcohol slip down my throat and warm me inside.

"Permission to take your cabin boy, Captain?" Ezra asked, his tone sardonic and dry as the wine tasted.

Tate chuckled. "Of course, just don't wear him out entirely, First Mate. I'd rather like to take him myself later on."

I blushed and told myself it was just the wine taking effect. I wasn't humiliated by talk of sex these days, but these two making a joke out of it, and of my formal manner, well. It was a little more humiliating.

I drank again from the wine bottle and handed it back to

Tate, smacking my lips. Ezra offered me his arm, as if he were a
gentleman and I was a fine lady.

"It's as if you've been at the rum already," I said, huffily, and
took his proffered arm. He might be making fun of me, but I still
loved him and wanted to see what he had planned.

CHAPTER TEN - IN WHICH GIDEON'S TRAINING IS FURTHERED

He led me some way off from the group, and back into the trees a little. We walked until we were out of direct sunlight and to a flattish bit of land.

Ezra turned to me and before I could react, he twisted his arm under mine and grabbed my wrist, forcing it up behind my back, his other hand going to my hip to push me towards the nearest coconut palm trunk.

I gasped, hardly able to register what he'd done until my cheek was pressed against the smooth bark.

"Been too long since we were truly alone, hasn't it, pet?" He growled, his teeth finding the tender skin just below my ear and biting so that I grunted.

"Oh, God. Yes," I said, closing my eyes.

He twisted my arm further up my back and I bit down a cry of protest. "What do you call me, *pet*?"

I gasped and screwed my eyes shut - how could I have forgotten that already?

"Master. Sorry, Master."

"Mmm. That's better. Don't move." He let go of my hip and I drew a slow and shaky breath. The rough handling had me halfway to an orgasm already, and the urge to rut against the tree like some kind of sex-crazed beast was throbbing through me.

I resisted, but perhaps only because Ezra still held my arm up my back. I concentrated on the burn of the twist in my arm, and controlling my breathing.

He slipped my leather collar around my neck and let go of my arm so he could buckle it closed. I let my arm fall back into a more comfortable position.

He must've had the collar in his pocket, I wonder what else he brought with him?

I was getting used to the feel of it now, and more so, the meaning that it held. While I wore the collar I wasn't to argue with him. I was to be a good pet, and obey him.

Although, I could still tell him if he crossed into behaviour I didn't like, or caused me too much pain, but I was to serve him as long as I was comfortable.

I felt my racing heart slow down a bit. The comfort of the familiar. Ezra tugged me back from the tree and looked me up and down. "Take your clothes off. Then mine."

"Of course, yes Master." I quickly unfastened my shirt and set it aside, my fingers trembling as I undid my trousers and pulled them off, then went to do the same to the black shirt and pants Ezra wore.

As I worked, I allowed myself to look at him, really notice all the small details and aspects of him I might not usually see. His Adam's apple was slightly red, as if he'd scraped himself shaving. He had a small white scar on his chest, just above his left nipple. His breath smelled of rum.

His hair was perfect, a pompadour on top, and shaved at the sides of his head. It made him look like a magnificent warrior, and I loved how much attention he gave it, the care he put into his appearance.

Once I had removed his trousers, he smiled a slow and wicked smile.

"Now, pet, today's lesson will be patience. How do you think you will do?"

Oh stars, what does that mean? He's not going to tie my cock with leather again is he? That was absolute torture.

"I can be patient," I said, although my voice hitched as I said it, betraying my uncertainty. I dropped my eyes, looking at his gorgeous, heavy cock standing out from the dark thatch of hair down there.

I could be, I just didn't *want* to be much of the time.

Ezra laughed. "Well, we'll see, won't we? Go to the tree and put your hands on the trunk, up over your eye level. Your hands aren't to move from that position."

I swallowed and turned back to the tree, reaching up to put my hands on the smooth bark, quite close to each other so my thumbs touched, and rested my forehead on the backs of them, bracing myself for whatever was to come. For I had no doubt he was going to draw this out.

"Like this, Master?"

"Just like that," Ezra said. He moved closer, pressing his hardness against me for the barest moment.

I whined, wanting more, and Ezra chuckled darkly. "I haven't even started, pet. What I'm going to do is tease you, and you are not to come, do you understand? Let's see how much composure you can keep. And leave your hands there, or I'll have to bind them."

"I do like it when you bind me," I said, softly, against the bark of the tree.

Ezra brushed my hair to one side, letting it fall to the front of my shoulder, out of his way, and he bit the back of my neck, sinking his teeth in around the leather of the collar until I groaned.

He pressed himself against me, pinning me to the tree, but it was another tease, a promise with no follow through. He pulled back and I heard movement. I turned my head but I couldn't see him without letting go of the tree, which I didn't dare to do.

Before I could take a breath, I felt his hand on my back, fingers slick with oil, dabbing it down my spine and letting it drip into the crack of my rear.

I shivered with need, but I was determined that I'd do as he asked. I would stay still and be good. I could be patient if that's what Ezra wanted of me.

I did step my feet a little farther apart though, as that felt like it would be helping him rather than disobeying.

"That's a good boy," Ezra said, and I felt gratified in my choice. He slipped his slick finger between my cheeks and started to probe at me.

I could never get used to that sensation, it was wonderful every time. So deeply intimate and pleasurable. The sting of him pushing his finger inside was instantly replaced with delectable sensations of need. Heat flashed through my body.

"Like that, do you?" he crooned in my ear.

"Ye-yes, Master."

He gently pulled his finger out of me and then pushed it back in, a mimic of what I hoped he'd soon be doing with his cock. Over and over.

My breathing became heavier, faster, whining deep in my throat as he continued in exactly the same manner, not increasing speed or depth at all. It was incredibly good, but it wasn't enough to come from.

On the verge of begging him, I suddenly realised what it was he was doing. *This* was the training.

Learning how to take and be teased, without reaching completion. My breath caught and I moaned out a soft "oh."

"That's right, caught on now, have you pet?" Ezra bit my shoulder gently. I assumed that meant approval.

"You wish me to be patient," I gasped. "To take what I am given and no more, yes?"

"That's it, such a clever lad," he said, and softly bit the back of my neck below the collar.

I flushed with happiness at the praise and closed my eyes.

But I soon discovered that closing my eyes made it worse, because it put more of my attention on Ezra's fingers. I gasped and moaned softly, trying to quiet myself although it seemed impossible to do so.

He hasn't actually told me to be quiet, at least. Just to take it...

He sped up without warning, fucking his fingers in me faster and faster until I was moaning loud, sure I was about to orgasm.

Then, just as I felt the crest of it, his fingers stilled inside me, and the sensation eased off. It was close, very close, and my cock was throbbing with it, but I wouldn't be able to come unless he fucked me again or stroked me.

"Ohhhhh," I said, realising all over again.

He meant to torture me, that was the intention. Of course it was. It was a constant revelation how much he enjoyed torture, and in my turn how I enjoyed his cruelty so much...

"Good boy," he said. And his fingers started to move once more, gently, teasingly shallow inside me. "This is your first lesson in edging. Can you guess why it's called that?"

I swallowed hard, finding it hard to concentrate on thinking while the waves of delicious tension washed through me let alone form a sentence. But he'd asked, and he expected an answer. Which meant something, didn't it? Right, words he wanted me to say words to him.

Could I guess the answer?

"Uh, no Master," I said finally.

"Because I'm going to keep you on the edge, but not quite letting you over," he murmured. He started to finger me faster, his fingers pushing in and out, dragging against the tender ring of me and sparking sensation through my body. I was surely loose enough for his cock now but I didn't think he'd give me that in any hurry.

I whined, biting hard on my lip as my need to orgasm built up from his fingers. He must've felt me tensing around him, because his fingers stilled, leaving my blood pounding through my body and my breath rasping from my throat. Caught on the edge of everything and unable to tip over unless he let me - made me.

"Please, Master, please," I gasped. His fingers slipped from me, and I tried to turn to him, to press myself against him and beg harder for release.

He chuckled and let me turn, looking me in the eyes. His eyes were crinkled with amusement, and I thought - affection. "Want something, pet?"

"Please, yes, I'm so close," I said, although I could feel the sensations ebbing away again as he wasn't touching me.

"Get down on the ground, on your front, but push your arse up, present it to me," he said.

I was past the point of finding such an order humiliating. All I could think of was him touching me more, getting me to completion and how much I positively ached for it. So I went down on my hands and knees and pushed my rear towards him.

He knelt beside me, buried his hand in my hair and pushed my head down so my chest was on the ground.

"Hands out in front of you," he grunted, and I did as he said.

"That's a good pet. Very good. Now, hold that position." He spanked me once with a hard hand and then slipped his fingers back into me making me gasp. His other hand remained in my hair, tugging it deliciously with the tightness of his grip, while still using it to push me down to the ground.

I wasn't bound at all, but I felt I couldn't move from where he put me. I didn't want to anger him, or do anything to make him at all displeased, besides both of his hands were rather insistent and I was enjoying them. If I moved I might dislodge them.

The need inside me became all consuming as he crooked his finger and pressed at a certain spot inside me. The pleasure welled up and I felt my skin flush hot, sweat beading on my forehead and I cried out.

"Aah! Please, Master, please!"

He chuckled and eased his finger off the spot, instead very gently massaging around my hole, and then toying with my testicles. It was so much, too intense. The sound of waves crashing seemed to fill my hearing - something I needed but was out of reach. I closed my eyes and willed myself to hold still although I wanted to thrash and buck my hips.

"Just a little longer, Gideon." His voice cut through the roaring sound and grounded me back in my body, back with Ezra. I focused on his voice and whined again. Feeling utterly beyond speaking unless it was to beg.

He shifted behind me, pushed my legs apart and started to tease me with his cock instead of his fingers. I felt tears squeezing out from between my eyelids. "Please Master please," I repeated. "Please, please."

The waves crashing filled my head again, and I moaned, pushing every so slightly back against the velvet softness of his cock. I wanted it so bad I was salivating, in danger of drooling like a baby if I opened my mouth too wide.

"Still now, pet," he said, in that same soft tone.

I'd do absolutely anything for that voice.

I willed my body to freeze, to be as stone. He pushed himself inside agonizingly slowly and in some way, everything felt as new and as intense as it had my very first time with Tate.

It was as if my skin had never been touched by a man, as if my rear had never opened to take a cock before.

Heat pooled in my stomach and then spread through me. My fingers dug into the soft, sandy ground and I opened my eyes again, focusing on the nearest tree and tensing as he pushed deeper, wanting to prolong every sensation myself, now.

"Try to relax," he said. "Accept what you're feeling, don't fight the sensations. It's intense, I know, but you'll thank me at the end."

Slowly he pushed himself deeper inside and I tried to understand what it was he meant.

Don't fight them, accept them. Well, what was I feeling?

A need, an aching, crushing need to reach completion.

Desire to please Ezra, to hear him praise me again.

So much goodness, so much fiery lust and desire I feared it might consume me.

Accept it, don't fight.

I breathed out deeply, telling myself everything that was happening to my body wasn't bad, that it wasn't a stress on me, instead, I focused on the pleasure of it.

I liked pleasure, obviously. And Ezra was giving me so much of it. Drawing it out of me slowly instead of all at once.... I could only imagine what this was leading to.

The whine in my throat turned into a deep, satisfied moan and my body relaxed somewhat.

"That's it, good, perfect boy, so good for me," Ezra said. He let go of my hair and stroked his hand down my back instead, and I practically purred. If I'd been Zeb I would have.

I took another deep breath and moaned again as Ezra pushed deep inside me.

The desire to orgasm had transformed from a threatening wave that wanted to crash over me, now it was more akin to riding a boat on the ocean as it swelled. Up and down, pleasant, but not dangerous. The desperation leaked out of me and I came to feel at one with my body, with Ezra, who was part of me in some way, and with the way I was feeling.

"Now, I'm gonna fuck you until you come, got it?" Ezra asked. Although I could feel him inside me, his voice sounded curiously distant.

Now that I'd adjusted to it, I didn't feel the need to come, in fact, I thought I could hold on with a lot more teasing if that's what he wanted to give me.

I must have made a kind of noise that indicated some of this, because Ezra chuckled, curled his fingers and scratched my back.

"Aye, maybe you're enjoying it now, but Goddamnit it all, Gideon. You're too gorgeous, and I'm gonna get off inside you, and nothing feels as good as when you come at the same time as me."

Well, I could hardly argue with that reasoning.

He started to roughly thrust inside me, pulling and pushing and slamming into me. His hand found my cock and started to pump it in time with his thrusts and I was reduced to panting and grunting under him.

Before long, my body was tensing, apparently the ability to hold off, bobbing on the ocean of it, couldn't withstand the roughness of Ezra's cock.

"Come for me, pet," he grunted, and I could feel that he was on the verge himself.

I didn't need telling twice, I bucked under him and my cock spurted against my stomach and over the sand. I clenched down hard on him and he filled me, hot and wet. He cried out, less a moan of happiness and more a victory cry.

He pulled out slowly and I could feel his spending leaking out of me. I felt boneless, my knees giving out until I was lying totally prone. Ezra gently turned me on my side, moved so I could lean against him as he lay down behind me and put his arms around me.

I wanted to speak but I wasn't capable, I'd seen stars and suns, the light glinting off the imaginary sea I'd been sailing on, my throat was dry and my mind utterly blank, at peace.

Ezra's arms were snug around me, and his lips pressed gently against my shoulder as I tried to gather myself.

Eventually these feelings faded somewhat and I was able to

breathe normally, form sentences in my mind and even turn a little to smile at him.

"So, that's edging," Ezra said. "How did you like it, as if I couldn't tell?"

"Incredible," I said, smiling wider. "I mean, I don't think I would want that every time, but my God, it was… it was something utterly transformative."

Ezra laughed and squeezed me against him. "Never change, Gideon. You're an odd one but I…" He inhaled and looked away. "I like you a lot. I might have even fallen for you."

My breath caught. I was easy enough with my love, giving it and expressing it easily to all my lovers, but Ezra had not yet managed to say those words back to me. Perhaps his time on the Trinity Royal had clarified some things for him?

I turned a bit more until I was lying on my back, looking up at him. I pushed up to kiss him softly, I didn't want to push him past what he was comfortable with emotionally. Instead, I could be patient and wait until he was ready.

"I love you Ezra," I said softly. "Thank you so much."

"For what?" He asked, one side of his mouth pulling up.

"For being you, for being my Master," I said. "And for this, it was astounding, truly."

He kissed me again, a more sensual, warm kiss than his usual battle for control and I wrapped my arms around his neck and lost myself in it.

CHAPTER ELEVEN - IN WHICH ROGUES
REVEL

When Ezra and I made our way back to the beach, the party was already in full swing, although the sun had barely dipped towards the horizon. There was a roaring bonfire on the sand, and sausages and bread were being toasted on long sticks - filling the air with savoury smells that made my mouth water.

Ora was sitting near the water's edge with Zeb, and they appeared to be sharing a bottle of wine. Tate was easy to spot - his laughter rang loud and deep over the sound of waves and the crackle of the fire.

Thinking not to interrupt Ora and Zeb, I approached the group where Tate was, I thought I saw Zack in there, and wanted to make sure he wasn't too overwhelmed by the activities.

"There you are, Gid," Tate exclaimed. He shoved a bottle of rum into my hands and I gamely took a swig, although I was still not used to the burn of the stuff.

"Here I am, indeed," I said. Tate wrapped an arm around me and pulled me against his side.

"Did Ezra wear you out?" He kissed the top of my head as I took another swig of rum. It seemed Tate was very merry, and I wanted to be there with him.

"No, he didn't," I said. I tilted my head and pushed up on my toes to kiss Tate. "I'm fine."

"That's very good to hear. Thank you, First Mate!" Tate shouted, and took the rum bottle back so he could raise it in a toast to Ezra, who saluted back from the fire, where he was snagging some toasted bread.

"We were about to tell some stories," Tate said.

"Food first!" Sagorika called. She pulled a large pot from the embers at the edge of the bonfire and pulled the lid off. It was another of her delicious curries and my stomach rumbled all over again. "Grab a bowl and form a line."

I pulled out from under Tate's arm and hurried to join the line. Zack had a huge ladle and made quick, efficient work of serving the somewhat tipsy pirates, and then me.

"How's things?" I asked Zack as he filled my bowl with a fragrant ladleful.

"Good," Zack said. "This is so much fun. Do you know Ora showed me how they swim in the shallows? It's so different to what I was taught."

"I'm glad you're getting on with them," I said, meaning it. A little of my apprehension over how Zack would settle in alleviated.

"Now go eat," Zack said, laughing. "You're holding up the line."

I glanced behind me to see Tate and Ezra both behind me, holding bowls, and laughed a little. "Right, thank you."

I went back up the beach where someone had dragged some logs and took a seat on one of the bigger ones, leaving plenty of room for Tate.

Soon enough, we were all eating happily and telling Sagorika and Zack how good the food was.

"This is the last time I'm cooking for you for a long while," Sagorika said. "I've been doing too much of it, and I'm done!"

"But you're the best at it," James grumbled.

"Everyone takes their turn," Tate said. "It must be my turn, I can't remember the last time I cooked."

I smiled and turned to him. "What kind of things do you cook? I can't recall you cooking since I joined the Grey Kelpie."

"Definitely your turn, then," Ezra said.

"Well, I do a little fish stew, some scones, maybe a meatloaf if we have provisions," Tate said.

"It's none of it very tasty," Ezra murmured, leaning closer to me.

I stifled a giggle.

"More rum?" Tate passed the bottle back to me and I chased my mouthful down with more of the liquor. It was starting to taste better to me, and I found I enjoyed the warming sensation as it slipped down my gullet.

Once the food was finished, Zack was prodded and coaxed into telling us a story, as the newest to the ship, he was most likely to have stories none had heard before.

"Given your ship's name, you may've heard stories about kelpies before," Zack started, his voice uncertain. "But you'll not have heard this one, as it comes from my very own grandmama..."

This was met with enthusiastic cheers, so Zack straightened his back and continued with more confidence.

"Grandmama was just a young thing, barely sixteen and she were gathering herbs and suchlike down by the river when a startlingly handsome young man appeared to her. He had golden hair, long down his back and a fine bearing."

There were some whoops and rumbles from the audience.

"Sounds like you, Gideon!" Tate cried, and elbowed me hard enough I fell a little into Ezra and laughed as I righted myself.

"My hair's not *golden*," I said.

Zack shook his head, laughed a little and continued. "He

told her she was beautiful and asked to lay with her and as he sat beside her she was enamoured, and saw only the beauty of him and the way the dappled sunlight caught in his hair.

"You mayn't lay with me, she told him, for they were unwed, but he might sit awhile with her as she found wild garlic in the shallows of the river. He agreed and sat beside her, all the while telling her lovely things about her beautiful eyes and her long hair. She was well pleased, and imagined how she would bring him home to her folks and they could arrange an engagement - although she'd never seen the man before and had no idea where he came from."

Zack paused to take a drink of wine. The crew had gone largely silent, caught in the images of the story Zack shared, and tense as we waited for the conflict to play out, as it was surely coming.

Zack burped quietly then continued. Ora moved up to sit at my feet, leaning their back against my legs, I played with their hair with one hand.

"She pulled up a bulb of garlic, leaning forward for a moment, and when she turned back she caught sight of two things. One was the man watching her with a wide smile, one full of sharp teeth." He paused for affect, pulling his own mouth into a frightening grimace.

Some people listening shivered and murmured at that, but honestly, it just made me think of Ora. I was a little afraid of what Ora could do in their true form, and their tendency to eat people - but I knew that I had nothing to fear from my darling merfolk, they'd no sooner hurt me than Tate would. I trusted them utterly.

"What was the other thing?" Sagorika called out.

"The other thing was a strand of green river weed caught in the lad's hair. Now, grandmama knew her lore. She knew instantly that river weed in the hair of a handsome lad or lass spelled only one thing, a water horse or kelpie. And this one wanted to lay with her, which meant he wanted to entrap her and draw her down into the water.”

Ora chuckled a little. Ezra eyed them with uncertainty. I kept on playing with their hair, pulling it back and starting to braid it.

“So, what was she to do? She had no weapon, nothing to make a bridle with, only the silver necklace with the cross she wore around her own neck. Which would work all right perchance, but how could she convince the kelpie to put it around his own neck? She didn’t panic though, she let on nothing of what she knew and sat back in her place, stripping the leaves off the garlic and setting it in her basket.”

Zack took another drink.

“She should’ve fucked him!” James shouted, then fell over on his side, laughing. Anton shook his head.

“Don’t stop now, Zack! I want to know what happened!” He called.

“Well, she sat for a time and spoke sweet things right back to the kelpie, although he was starting to get impatient, moving closer to her and trying to touch her waist and she kept on edging away from him. Being careful of course, to move up the bank and away from the water instead of into it - fearing that if she was too close to the river, the kelpie would just lunge forward and drag her under. In any case, the kelpie started to whine. ‘I just want to be with you, bonnie lass,’ and so on. So finally, she got angry and turned to him and said ‘I cannae be with a man I’m not betrothed to’ and he said ‘so betroth us’ clearly not knowing what it meant. She told him it would mean just the two of them together for all time, and he agreed readily. ‘Then wear this: a symbol of our union,’ she said, and unfastened her necklace.”

Ezra slipped his arm around my waist and I thought of the leather collar he had given me, that I could almost still feel around my neck like a promise. I leaned against him as I braided the last bit of Ora's hair.

"The kelpie bowed his head and allowed her to put the silver cross on him, although once it was fastened he hissed in pain, as if it burned him. 'Are you all right?' my grandmama asked, and the kelpie nodded. 'Now you will lay with me, I don't mind being bound to you if I can have you. I've seen you so many times, and loved you since the first moment I saw you, and this is the first time I've been brave enough to tell you so.' Then she took him back home with her, and they were married within a month, although Grandmama told me they bedded that night, and most every night since then as well. The kelpie's monstrous form was lost to him, although the rumour in the family is that we all inherited a bit of his charm and a bit of his luck."

With that, Zack bowed to signify the story's end and the crew all laughed and clapped.

Zack smiled wide at the warmth of the applause, drained the last of his wine and went for a refill.

Anton got up to tell the next story.

Ora turned to smile up at me. "Thanks for doing my hair. Do you want to go for a walk? Promise I won't drag you into the water and drown you." I chuckled and stood up.

"It would be my absolute pleasure," I wobbled a bit on my feet, the rum I'd been sipping had taken more of an effect than I'd anticipated.

"Careful, Gid," Tate said, laughing. He slapped me on the rear and my face flushed, but that could have easily have been from the rum or from the proximity to the fire.

Ora took my hand and we walked away from the group as Anton began his tale. I glanced over my shoulder at Tate and winked at him, promising without words I hadn't forgotten that he'd said he wanted some time with me that night.

I saw Zeb stretched out on the far side of the fire, his belly exposed to the heat, apparently fast asleep.

"The amount of time he spends asleep," I murmured. "I thought that was just a cat thing."

"He is still a cat," Ora said, squeezing my hand. "His form doesn't change that, he still has many of the same instincts."

"I'd noticed."

I bumped my shoulder against Ora's and chuckled. "We're going towards the waves, are you sure you're not planning on drowning me?"

"Oh, we're going into the water. Sex is amazing in the water," Ora said. "But I won't *drown* you."

Warmth spread through my belly and I bumped my shoulder against theirs again. "You did have nefarious plans for me, I should have known."

"Nefarious?"

"You know, like, wicked," I grinned at Ora. In the light of the setting sun, their pale skin was painted orange and golden, utterly lovely.

Ora smiled back at me, surely mirroring the expression of adoration I'm sure I was wearing. The sand under my bare feet was warm but not hot, my stomach was full and I felt full of freedom, love and contentment.

We walked into the water, letting the waves lap at our feet and ankles. Ora walked deeper but I stopped.

"Wait, I should take my clothes off, first," I said. "And so should you, leave them on the shore so they'll stay dry."

"I don't mind them wet," Ora said, but we both stripped all the same and tossed our clothes back up to the dry sand.

I spared a glance towards the bonfire, but no one there seemed concerned about our sudden nakedness. Too distracted, or perhaps, too accustomed to it now?

Whatever the reason, it didn't matter.

Ora splashed into the deeper water and I followed - the water was pleasantly warm, almost like a bath, and I hurried to catch up and throw myself into their arms where the water was about waist height.

Being with just Ora was so different to being alone with Ezra. Ezra made demands, forced my body into situations and I had to keep on thinking with him. None of which was a bad thing, but with Ora the two of us understood each other on such a fundamental level I didn't have to think or consider. I just let my body do what it would.

Ora caught me in their arms and kissed me passionately, tangling their tongue with mine in just the way I liked. I moaned into their mouth and pressed my chest against theirs.

"A little deeper," Ora murmured and lifted me in their arms. I wrapped my legs around their waist as they walked deeper in. I kissed my way up their jaw and nipped under their ear.

"How do you want to do this?" I asked, softly. Ora and I took turns as the one being fucked and the one fucking, and I loved it both ways.

"Since you're already in position…" Ora's hand slipped behind me to tease me where Ezra had fucked me an hour earlier. The salt water stung a little, but I was still stretched and open for it. I moaned, their fingers felt good, stirring up the ache of Ezra's pounding earlier in the best way.

With little more prep Ora slipped their cock inside me, pushing up and deep in without too much strain. The sensation was hot and cold, hot from the feel of Ora's skin, colder from the water. I closed my teeth on the shell of Ora's ear to stifle the louder groans I wanted to make.

Ora's hand was under my rear, holding me in place, and my ankles locked together around their waist. My arms around their neck.

"Let go," Ora half moaned. "With your arms, lean back. The water will hold you up."

I did as they said, letting go and leaning back until I was floating on the surface of the water, my legs wrapped around my lover, and their cock buried deep inside me. I groaned, the sensation of weightlessness was adding to the intensity of our lovemaking.

Ora's hand moved to my lower back, supporting me on the water as they began to rock their hips and thrust into me.

I let my arms stretch over my head, feeling the ocean holding me as Ora filled me again and again. It was a strange but wonderful way to make love.

I reached up to Ora, who leaned in to kiss me. Feeling a little light headed, I pulled them down towards me, and their feet left the ground, buoyed up by the swell of the waves. Ora wrapped their arms around me and rolled us so they were partially submerged and I was looking down on them, both of us floating horizontally.

I used the movement of the waves to guide me, pushing myself down against Ora's cock and moaning.

"Do you trust me?" Ora asked, softly. They leaned up, water streaming off their face and hair, and kissed me, salty and true.

"Of course I do," I said.

"Then let's try underwater, just for a moment," Ora said. They began to sink into the water, I suppose it was part of being merkind, or Ora's magic, but we slowly sank towards the sand. As the water swirled around my shoulders, I took a deep breath and closed my eyes.

The water all around us was warm and welcoming somehow. I felt no fear, because I trusted Ora and their magic, they were showing me something new, and I had come to realise how much I love new things.

My hair lifted off my neck and swirled around me and I opened my eyes, surprised when there was no salt sting, and I could see Ora quite well. I leaned in and kissed them again and they rolled us, pushing me further under and fucking me in earnest, possessing and enjoying me in equal measures. I held onto their biceps, loosened my legs from their waist to tangle their legs and took it.

It was difficult not to moan, and as we got closer, Ora rose us to the surface until our heads broke into the night air. I took a deep breath and moaned out loud, my hand moving to stroke myself as Ora thrust into me and reached completion. In a moment, I followed, marvelling at the different sensations the water gave me. How cool it felt and how like another caress the waves were.

Ora set their feet on the ground and I followed suit, leaning heavily on their chest as I caught my breath.

"So good..." I panted.

"I'm glad you liked it," Ora said. They smoothed my hair back from my face and wiped some water from my eyes. "I want it always to be good for you."

I flushed with happiness and kissed them again, winding my arms around their neck and pouring all my love and joy into the kiss. Ora returned it with enthusiasm, and it felt as if our souls were swirling in the sea around us, or possibly blowing in the gentle Bahamian breeze around our heads and rejoicing.

Ora finally broke the kiss and grinned at me. "D'you want me to give you a ride back to shore?"

It wasn't far, but I knew what they meant and I yes, I wanted it. On the first day we'd met, Ora had swum with me on their back and it had been exhilarating and terrifying in equal measure. We weren't far out so it wouldn't be too bad, besides I'd tangled with a sea witch and the British Navy since then.

And my experience under water just now had been rather pleasant.

"Yes, please."

Ora let go of me to shift into their merfolk form and then waited while I put my arms around their torso from behind. I linked my hands together around their chest and kissed their shoulder.

"I'm ready."

Then we were off, Ora diving under the water and beating their tail to speed us through the waves. Laughter bubbled up inside me, for I was truly enjoying the thrill of the ride this time, but I kept my mouth firmly closed to avoid swallowing sea water.

Ora came to a stop in the shallows, and I rolled off their back and smiled up at them, resting on the soft sand.

Ora kissed me again. "I love you," they said.

"I love you, so very much," I said, stroking my hand over their chest.

For a moment we just gazed at each other, then Ora pushed up on their hands. "I think I'll go for a longer swim, this lagoon is wonderful."

"Sounds good. I think we'll all be sleeping by the fire tonight, I can't imagine people going back to the ship," I said.

Ora nodded and kissed me quickly. "I'll see you soon."

They flicked their tail, there was a small splash and they were gone, faster than a dolphin.

I sat up, wrung the water out of my hair and then stood to find my clothes. The dip in the ocean had made me quite sober, and from the sounds of things I had to get drinking if I was to match the energy at the bonfire.

CHAPTER TWELVE - IN WHICH GIDEON GETS DRUNK AND DREAMS

The heat of the bonfire dried me off quickly, which I was glad for. It was a warm night but I didn't like the thought of looking like a drowned rat. Zeb had woken up and was drinking with Tate so I went to join them. They sat side by side on a fallen log someone must've rolled over at some point.

"Gideon!" Tate said. He slapped his knee and looked expectantly at me, and it took me a moment to realise he expected me to sit on his lap.

"I couldn't," I said, as if I hadn't just gone out into the water and had sex where people had probably been able to see me.

"You can." He leaned forward and grabbed my wrist, pulling me in to perch on his thigh. I licked my lips, unwilling to argue further. I could smell Tate now, sense the nascent desire in him and it stoked the embers of my own desire once again. I leaned against his chest and he passed me the bottle of rum.

I took a drink, and then another drink because the rum warmed my chest.

I drained the last of the bottle and Tate had to pull out another. He drank from it and then gave me the fresh bottle, which I drank to try to see if it tasted different to the other bottle.

"So," Tate said, nuzzling into my ear, his voice warm and as liquid as the rum. "What'd you and Ora do out there, as if I didn't know?"

"Well, you know," I said, feeling not exactly shy but as if I should be shy, or at least, play along with Tate and pretend to be shy. Zeb pulled a face at me, making me laugh.

"Tell me, Gid."

"They showed me how fun the water can be," I said, lightly as I could manage.

"How fun... the water... actually, I like the water too," Zeb said. "It has fish in it. Fish are fun to catch, I'm going to get lots of them tonight when they're all asleep."

"Do fish sleep?" I asked, tilting my head so it rested on Tate's. The rum had worked quickly to make my head fuzzy. Tate snaked his arm around my waist to hold me steady.

"Course they sleep," Tate said. "They'se all, they're all, y'know, tucked up in their little fish beds, aren't they?"

"You two are pathetic," Zeb said, swiping the rum bottle off me and swigging deeply from it. "Can't hold your rum."

"You're a cat!" Tate exclaimed, and then started to laugh. I joined him, because it was true and in that moment it did seem to be utterly ridiculous that Zeb was a man and a cat.

"I am!" Zeb stood up and threw the mostly empty rum bottle into the fire where it made a bit of a whoomph noise, and then the glass shattered. The others around the fire ducked and cried out.

"Careful Zeb!"

"I'm A CAT! AND YOU ALL WISH YOU WERE CATS!" He shouted.

"Zeb, Zeb," I hissed and lunged for his hand.

"Oop," Tate said, catching me before I landed face first in the sand. "Carefully, Giddy."

I caught hold of Zeb's hand. "You can't shout about being a cat, the Navy might hear you!"

Zeb sat down and shuffled towards us, leaning his back on Tate's legs. "I don't feel so good."

"S'the rum," Tate said. He reached over to ruffle his hand through Zeb's hair. "Cats aren't supposed to drink it."

I giggled and wrapped my arms around Tate's shoulders to hold myself up, and Zeb huffed.

"I'll show you what cats are supposed to do," he grumbled. I looked over to see his eyes flashing in the firelight and the pricked points of ears poking up through his dark hair.

He wiggled his hips from side to side, then pounced on the both of us, knocking Tate on his back on the sand, and me crashing on top of him. Zeb, of course, was on top of both of us, struggling to pin Tate down by the wrists with me trapped between them laughing helplessly.

I tried to move and Zeb fell sideways off my back and I scrambled out of the way, trying to catch my breath. Tate launched himself at Zeb and the two of them tussled on the sand for a moment, both of them trying to overpower the other.

I felt like I should do something, but I wasn't sure what.

Stop them? But they looked so incredibly hot trying to grab and restrain each other.

Help one of them? But which one? I didn't particularly want either Zeb or Tate to win…

Get in the middle? I considered… maybe it was that option I wanted.

I shifted onto my knees and tried to grab at Tate's arm, and Zeb noticed me and stopped trying to haul Tate onto his back and went to pin me instead.

It was a mess, frankly, the three of us, drunk on rum, rolling around in the sand and wrestling like… like… I have no idea what wrestles like that.

Tate managed to get free of the both of us and stand up, and he took a few desperate, staggering steps towards the tree line before Zeb tackled his legs and they both crashed to the sand again.

I was free, so I got up and moved closer to the tree line as well, finding the sand terribly uneven - I guessed Tate had been angling for a little privacy away from the bonfire. I got a few steps closer, almost to the tree line when Tate's arms around my waist swept me into the air. I kicked uselessly.

"Let me go!" I cried out.

"Never!" Tate responded, laughing and then the three of us tumbled to the soft sand under the trees.

Soon enough, our shirts were torn off and tossed away and trousers were being kicked away. Tate's chest was under my hands and I was kissing his shoulders and neck while Zeb's hands ran over my rear, and his finger found my well fucked-out hole. I moaned with pleasure and the sweet sting of it.

Zeb was half kneeling on Tate's legs and Tate used the angle he was at to slap Zeb's ass, making him yelp. Then he reached between to massage Zeb's balls and I moaned, my hand slipping down to stroke and pump at Tate's magnificent cock. I needed more than just my hand, I realised, my mind blurred and hot and muted by the rum.

I moved down Tate's body, pushing my face towards him. Zeb moved above me and turned around, his feet on either side of Tate's thighs. Tate sat up and buried his face in Zeb's ass. Zeb half stood, his hands on my back as I took Tate in my mouth.

I sucked and licked at him, savoring the salt, hot taste of him as he dripped anticipation - such a nice counterpoint to the sweet sting of the rum.

Zeb was moaning and almost howling, pushing himself back against Tate's tongue and digging his claw-like nails into the skin of my back, raking it and making me shudder. I felt Tate throb in my mouth and started to pull back. There was movement above me, Zeb shifted and caught me in his arms and pulled me off my knees. Tate's hands found my waist, turning me and pulling me close, between them they situated me in Tate's lap, my back to his chest, and with a deft hand Tate pushed himself inside me, letting me sink into place directly on his cock.

Somehow, Tate had his back to a tree trunk - had that always been there? The details had become hard to keep track of, especially when Zeb sank down on top of me, facing me and Tate with a self-satisfied expression of pleasure.

I gasped, my head spun in the best ways. I gripped Zeb's biceps and held on as the sensations of being filled utterly by Tate and buried deep inside Zeb at the same time threatened to overwhelm me.

Zeb kissed me, distracting me from my spiral and allowing me to focus on the pleasure rather than the overwhelming feeling. Tate's beard brushed my shoulder as he kissed my neck and I felt the three of us connecting on a deeper level, the magic inside me showing me the heat and light of our essences flowing one to the other.

Or... perhaps that was just the rum, again.

It didn't take long in that position for all of us to be on the edge of completion. Tate rolled his hips into me and that pushed me deeper into Zeb, who would respond by tensing his body, pulling himself up and then plunging down, which pushed me further onto Tate.

We were a tangle again, but this time we weren't fighting. We were moving together to create an incredible enjoyment of each other, a joy bigger than any of us could feel individually.

I was the first to reach completion, trapped between the two gorgeous men, both of them so much larger than me. I groaned against Zeb's shoulder and spent myself for the third time since we'd anchored the ship, mere hours before. I wrapped my hand around Zeb's cock and pumped him.

Tate was hard upon my heels, bucking hard against me and tilting his head back to cry out as he filled me with his seed.

Zeb rocked twice more on my cock and then spilled over my

hand and my chest. He rested his forehead against mine for a moment, and I felt the soft points of his cat ears poke against my hairline before he slowly toppled sideways off us and onto the sand.

Tate lifted me off him and set me down beside Zeb and the three of us stayed still, catching our breath and moaning with the aftershocks of the orgasms.

"Back to the fire," Tate rasped after a few minutes. "S'warmer."

"Right," I said. "Shirt?"

"Fuck it," Tate said, with emphasis. "Pants though. Pants."

He reached around in the dark and in a moment my trousers hit me in the face.

"S'fine here," Zeb yawned. "Just sleep right here."

"Zeb, Zeb," I said. "Think of the fire... so warm. Warm on your belly."

Zeb moved and I could hear him finding his own trousers.

"Good point." With some difficulty, primarily the sand being uneven and shifting under my feet and my body not liking being upright, the three of us somehow made our way back to the bonfire, where the story telling had started up again.

Tate settled down against the log, and I crawled into his lap to snuggle and Zeb stretched himself out over our legs. Warm and contented, I fell asleep as Sagorika told a story about a god coming down onto Earth and making trouble for some warriors.

I dreamed I was back on the Trinity Royal, standing out on the deck in the night, the stars above me and a cool wind blowing in my hair.

Across the deck, Captain Thornton stood, his back straight and his chin jutted out, the box from his office desk clutched in his hands. Light poured out from the lid as it opened on its own. The wind turned more violent, whipping my face.

I moved closer to him, called out as loud as I could. "Captain! Don't open it!"

A dark laugh echoed over the deck - a voice I knew. Not the Captain's... Not Tate's...

"Get out of here, Gideon," it said.

"Solomon," I hissed. I looked around for him, but there was nothing but the creaking of the ship, the stars above, the waves around us.

Captain Thornton didn't seem to have noticed me, he hadn't reacted to my cry.

The box opened fully and his face was bathed in a soft green glow. As I watched, disbelieving, the figure of Solomon coalesced on the deck before him, transparent and glowing with the same green light.

Solomon turned towards me. "Still here, are you? I've been having trouble tracking you for some reason... perhaps your barriers are down right now, though."

"What was that?" Captain Thornton looked up the deck but didn't seem to see me. "I need you to send a report."

"Tell me where you are, Gideon." He was right in front of me now, somehow in the blink of an eye moving from the captain to me.

Solomon reached to caress my cheek and I flinched, terrified, but I couldn't make myself move away from him. My feet were rooted to the deck.

"Show me where to find you, and where to find Tate. That's all I want."

I felt the answer rise in my throat - he had the ability to make someone speak the truth, I had experienced it before. I clenched my jaw shut and shook my head.

"Come on, tell me." His hand closed on my cheek.

I fought to stay silent, unable to move or to resist for much

longer at all... except there was something I was forgetting.
What was it?

"I say, come back here, what are you doing? I need to send a
message."

Captain Thornton? He couldn't help me. Couldn't even see
me. This was a dream, I realised.

Solomon can walk in dreams, and he has power in dreams.
He can turn people to his will, even give them objects, I knew all
of this. It meant I was in danger.

But he wasn't the only one with power, was he? The thing I
was forgetting rattled against my temple, willing me to
remember.

Something about power.

Dreams. He had magic that allowed him to walk in dreams.

Magic... that was it!

I have magic of my own, although I don't understand it. I
know it has something to do with sex and love, that's when I feel
it. I can't betray the men I love to the witch.

I called on the Heavens to let me access the magic inside me
and I felt a responding warm glow in my sternum.

Solomon's hand whipped back from my face like it had
burned him.

"What are you doing? Stop that at once."

His saying that was all the encouragement I needed. I
imagined Tate, and how much I wanted to protect him from
harm. I thought of Ezra and keeping him from the gallows, from
my father. Zeb and Ora, I conjured their faces in my head, let my
emotions fuel whatever the warmth was that Solomon didn't
like.

His face contorted into a mask of anger and he raised his
hands, there was something in them, something he was fiddling
with. I couldn't make it out. I knew on some level that it was a
bad thing, though, that I had to get away from this place.

With a huge effort of will, I turned away from Solomon and

focused entirely on the love I felt. I heard Solomon scream out a spell.

I woke up gasping.

Tate grumbled. I was lying with my head pillowed on his chest, his arm was around me, and Zeb was pressed against my back, making me almost uncomfortably warm. It was still dark, but the fire had burned down to embers. I watched the warm glow of them as my heart pounded.

I didn't think that had been just a dream.

I had somehow spied on The Trinity Royal, and Solomon had noticed, and spoken to me. More than that, he'd used his magic and tried to get me to betray our location. But I'd fought him off, got myself back safely.

I thought, anyway. I hoped.

I couldn't hear his voice any more, which was a good sign.

I tried to concentrate on the same warm sensations I'd felt in the dream when my magic had responded but it did nothing. I was warm, but it was because I was lying on and against two large warm men. I felt love for them, of course I did, but it didn't seem to bring the warm essence of magic to my hand.

Uncertain, I chewed my bottom lip. I thought I'd got away safely, but what if that spell he'd shouted had done something? Attached itself to me somehow? It would mean we weren't safe here for long.

I needed to tell the others what had occured, but I didn't want to wake them to do it. What if it was a false alarm?

I'd wait until morning, at least. I watched the embers, and puzzled over magic until I fell asleep again.

CHAPTER THIRTEEN - IN WHICH MAGIC IS PERFORMED

When I woke in the morning, I was too hot. My skin was clammy and my pants were drenched with sweat. I sat up and shivered, instantly feeling freezing. I wrapped my arms around myself as a tremble worked its way through my body.

It was only a little after dawn, and the others were still largely asleep, but I saw Ezra sitting up on the ocean side of the dead bonfire, looking out at the water.

Tate was snoring gently, and Zeb had, I think, noticed my stirring and ignored it, curling into a tighter ball than before.

I got to my feet and made my way over to Ezra, feeling unsteady, and shivering again.

He looked over at me and smiled softly. I sat beside him and shivered again, this one a more violent one, rattling my bones.

"You all right, Gideon?" He reached for his black coat and shook off the sand before draping it around my shoulders.

I smiled, pulling it closer around me. It smelled smoky and like Ezra. I wondered if he wore cologne or something because he had a scent to him that seemed to linger.

"I don't know, I had another dream with Solomon in it," I

said. "And I guess I'm hungover from the rum, I feel shivery and my muscles are aching."

"That doesn't sound like too much rum," Ezra said. "Too much rum would be a powerful ache in your head and queasiness in the belly." He reached over and placed a cool palm against my forehead. "Sounds like you might have a fever."

"A fever?" I pouted, it seemed unfair. Here I was on a beautiful beach with my favourite people in the world and I'd come down sick? At least I'd had plenty of fun the day before, I supposed.

Unless it was Solomon's doing...?

"Do you think Solomon could have made me sick?" I asked, in a small voice.

Ezra shrugged. "No idea, I don't understand the first thing about magic. But... to be honest, I wouldn't put it past him. Maybe we should talk to Ora."

I looked out at the ocean. "Have you seen them today?"

"I have not," he said. "But I'm sure they'll be along soon." He pulled me in against his side and put his arm around my shoulders. We sat like that for a while and I think I drifted off a little, because when Ezra spoke again I startled at the sound.

"There, I think I see Ora."

I caught my breath and licked my lips. I searched the waves and then made out the flicker of a black scaled tail. My heart lifted and I sat forward a bit as Ora swam closer to shore.

They shifted into human form in the shallows, wading in, and I got up to meet them.

"Careful," Ezra said. "You're sick and Ora's dripping wet."

"Right," I said, and pulled the coat further around me, I shivered again. "Morning, Ora."

"Morning love, is it true? You're sick? I hope that's not my fault for taking you swimming last night." Ora touched my hair and frowned.

"I don't know," I said. "I had a strange dream..."

Ora sat down and dripped dry in the morning sun and I told them and Ezra all the details I could remember from the dream, which was most of them. The dream had stayed quite clear in my head, which furthered my concern that the dream was truly magical and I had communicated with Solomon magically.

When I finished, I was shivering so hard my teeth rattled against each other.

Ezra frowned and put his arm around me again.

Ora tilted their head and looked me up and down. "Yes, I see it. It's not a curse exactly, but a spell is there attached somehow... like a limpet, stuck to your side."

I shuddered, that was a horrible image, a terrible sensation. I brushed at my arms as if I could scrub the spell off myself.

"Can you do something about it?" Ezra asked. Ora nodded and reached for my hands.

"Yes, and I think, I think Gideon can too, we just need to focus."

I squeezed Ora's fingers in mine and took a deep breath that rattled alarmingly in my chest. "Focus on what?"

"On the magic," Ora said, simply. As if that explained everything.

"I, uh, I-I'm not... I don't know..." I stammered.

"Just close your eyes and listen. And, if you can, join in..." Ora said. I closed my eyes and took another breath although it caught a little and I found myself coughing. I snatched my hand back from Ora to cover my mouth as the coughing got more insistent, more painful in my throat.

Ezra stood up. "I'm going to get him something to drink," he said. I watched as he walked back to where the crew were stirring.

"Please, let's try it again," Ora said. I nodded and took their hands again, closing my eyes as Ora started to hum. I tried to place the notes and once I thought I had the tune of their melody I hummed as well, although my voice sounded weak in comparison.

As we hummed together I felt something. The warm fire inside me, it was weak, as if it were just the starting flame of a fire, in need of tending and kindling, but it was there.

As Ora sang, switching from a hum to some language I didn't know, I felt it warm - as if Ora's voice was kindling. My own hum faltered as the scratch in my throat got worse. I cleared my throat and continued but as the flame glowed warmer, the urge to cough increased.

Once more, I broke contact with Ora to cover my mouth and cough. It felt as if something were stuck in my throat.

The coughing subsided after a minute, my eyes were streaming and my face felt hot. I felt inexplicably exhausted after the coughing fit, even though it couldn't have taken that much out of me.

Ora frowned. "That was working, I think. Yes, it was. Could you feel it?"

I nodded, not quite trusting myself to speak, feeling utterly miserable.

Ora huffed and reached for my hands. "We have to try again. It's trying to hold onto you. Come on, I know you can do this Gideon."

"Mrrp!"

I looked around to see Zeb in his black cat form trotting along the sand towards me, tail up and bent a bit just at the top.

"Zeb?" I croaked, then swallowed again.

Zeb crawled into my lap and started purring loudly. Ora smiled, meeting Zeb's eyes and tilting their head to the side.

"I think he might be able to help, he's magic, too, after all."

I stroked Zeb from ears to tail, feeling grateful for the heat of him on my legs, although not very hopeful at how he could help. I couldn't get through the music without coughing, and a cat couldn't stop that, magic or not.

I took Ora's hands and squeezed their fingers. "Once more."

This time I tried to hum immediately when Ora started the spell up, for I was relatively sure now that they were weaving a spell. Much of Ora's magic came from their siren voice.

Again, I felt the fire trying to flower into life inside me. This time I put all my focus on it, trying my best to sing it into being. In my lap, Zeb purred louder, and I felt the fire respond to that, flickering brighter, hotter in my chest.

Ora switched from notes to words and the fire responded to that too.

Thinking of the dream the night before, I let my attention waver from the fire and onto my love for Ora and for Zeb. Sparks flew off the fire and it warmed again. But as the song continued it didn't get any larger.

There's something wrong, something I'm not doing right, or something missing perhaps. If only I understood more about this...

A hand closed on my right bicep, fingers wrapping around it in a steel grip that should have all rights been frightening, except that I knew instantly it was Ezra. His strange expression of love, giving me affection and possessing me at the same time. His need to control, and take care of me seemed to flow through my arm and fed the fire.

On the other side of me, a warm, large hand spread against my left shoulder blade. Tate. Tate's warmth, his humour and his easy tenderness. His love, which was open and also hiding something deeper, something from his past, flowed into my back and straight into the flames.

I almost laughed out loud, my eyes flying open with joy as the fire crackled and sparked, the heat spread through my limbs, setting my blood aflame. I felt each connection point to one of my lovers as a white light, a beacon of hope and protection, which the flame fed on and then flowed back into.

The sensation of being a connection point between them all was heady, as if I were the center of the universe. I closed my eyes again and centralised my thoughts and emotions onto this feeling of convergence.

Ora's song reached a crescendo and I felt the fire burn brighter still.

I concentrated as hard as I could manage on being present, on connecting my lovers in flame and magic, and allowing them to love me in their own ways, and loving them with as much passion as I could summon.

Ora stopped singing, and I opened my eyes to see them looking at me with so much love it caught my breath. I cleared my throat and found I hardly needed to. The painful lump had gone.

Ezra and Tate let go of me and Zeb sat up in my lap to nuzzle his soft furry head under my chin. I stroked my hand down his soft, fuzzy back.

"Did it work?" Tate asked. I took stock of my body. The aches were gone, the shivers had vanished and all that was left was a bone-deep weariness.

"I think so," I said, and my voice sounded clear and steady to my own ears.

Ora nodded, leaned in and kissed me. "Yes, it worked perfectly. Better than I expected, especially once you two joined in. Three, rather," Ora added after Zeb mewed impatiently.

"It was all of us together," I said. "Could any of you feel it?"

"I... my hand tingled," Ezra said. I turned to look at him, picked up his hand and kissed his fingertips. "And... I suppose it felt good, somehow."

"I felt love," Tate said confidently. "I could feel you all, and Gideon especially, loving." He shook his head and laughed. "It was quite something, wouldn't mind doing that again."

Zeb hopped off my lap and rubbed against first Ora, then Tate, then Ezra, purring loudly.

"I felt it, too," Ora said. "The five of us, we're directly linked through Gideon. I think we have been for a while, but... this is the first time I've understood it on a bigger scale. We're linked by the universe, or by some higher power."

I smiled, feeling wrapped in warmth and love, and utterly exhausted.

"I think I need to rest," I said. "If that's quite all right with everyone?"

"Do you need anything? We brought you a drink," Tate said, offering me a bottle. I looked at it dubiously.

"Not more rum."

"It's water," he said, winking at me. I took the bottle and drank from it gratefully.

"Let's get you to a bed, maybe on the ship?" Ezra said. I set the bottle down in the sand and shook my head.

"No, I'd like to stay on the beach, if that's all right? I don't want to be too far from any of you."

"I'll send Anton to get blankets from the ship and pillows," Tate said. "We'll make you a little tent."

And so, within an hour, I was relaxing in great comfort in a quickly erected sunshade canopy. The front of the tent was open to the ocean, and I lay on a pile of blankets and cushions and dozed contentedly.

I was lulled by the sound of seagulls and waves in my ears. Every so often the burst of laughter from one of the crew made me smile.

When I was awake, I watched Ora and Zeb play in the shallows together, trapping fish, until eventually Zeb - back in his human form now - brought an armload of fish to the place the bonfire had been the night before.

Ezra and Tate were examining plans of the ship not too far away from me, and directing the crew to do repairs. They should, by all rights, be doing the repairs as well - as should I - but Tate had assured me that there would still be plenty to do on the morrow, and that today it was all right for me to rest and for them to stay near me.

Once work groups were dispatched back to the Grey Kelpie, the two of them started cleaning and gutting the fish, laying out fillets on baskets woven from coconut palm fronds.

Although I did want to be useful, I had accepted that after the spell and the curse before that, my body needed to rest and restore itself. I felt at peace with things, as if I had come to know myself in a new and better way.

When I fell asleep this time, my dreams were very different.

I woke in a bed in a bedroom, with sunlight streaming through light gauze curtains. The bed was gigantic, wider than I was tall by a few feet, and I knew it could comfortably fit all my lovers, and withstand any roughhousing or ... other group activities we might partake in.

None were there with me that morning, the sun was high in the sky - I must have overslept - so I got out of bed and walked down the hall. The floorboards were fresh and new under my feet, the house smelled pleasantly of new paint and sawdust.

I walked through the large, light filled kitchen to find a garden, newly planted but full of potential. Herbs and flowers, vegetables to the left and strawberry plants on a bed of straw, promising fruit already.

Ora knelt in the soil, tending herbs.

"Morning, love," they said. "It's a bit different to the seaweed gardens, but I think I can make it work."

I kissed them good morning. "You can make it work," I said, confident and assured.

I walked up the path around to the front of the house, where the verandah gave way to a patch of grass, and then to a bank covered in trees, sloping down to give us a view of the ocean. The blue green water moved faintly, sparkling in the light.

Tate sat at the table he'd set on the verandah, writing in a book. Not just any book - his journal, the log of the house instead of the ship. His account of the comings and goings, of what we needed and what he was feeling.

I walked up behind him and slipped an arm around his shoulder, kissed his head.

"You're awake?" Tate said, turning to smile at me. "I thought you'd sleep all day, after last night…"

I shook my head, pushed my hair behind my ears and smiled back. "I'm all right."

"Zeb's through there, in his favourite spot," he said, nodding through the open French doors and into the living space. I kissed him on the lips then let go and walked through. There, just as Tate had said, I found Zeb sprawled on the sofa.

We had three large sofas, arranged in a U shape so that you could look at the view no matter where you sat. It was where we spent our evenings. Whiling the time away singing songs, listening to Ezra play music, telling stories, drinking, or simply sitting and enjoying the silence together.

I sat beside Zeb, who was in his human form, although his ears were out, and his tail, showing how relaxed and happy he was. I stroked his hair and kissed the tips of his ears, making him smile and squirm. He put his arms around my waist and purred loud enough to rumble against my thigh.

"Love you," he murmured, mostly asleep.

"I love you, too, kitten."

"Mmm not a kitten."

After a time, he rolled away and I rose, knowing exactly where to find my final lover. The stairs that led down to the basement level echoed with the sound of a hammer, and I smiled.

Ezra had been working on this project since the main house was completed.

I walked down the stairs and cleared my throat so he'd not be surprised by my presence.

He set the hammer down and turned to me, handsome as ever, his hair disheveled and his forehead glistening from the exertion.

"Gideon. The cross is almost done," he said, and nodded to the contraption he was building. An X shaped rack with chains at each point, named a St Andrew's Cross. My cock stirred and I went to press myself against him.

"I can't wait," I said. Ezra's dungeon would soon be usable and then we would have such nights...

CHAPTER FOURTEEN - IN WHICH THE GREY KELPIE DOCKS IN NASSAU

For two more days we stayed in that isolated bay, repairing the ship as we could and eating more fish than we could stand. Ora and Zeb between them could catch so many, we ate like kings.

I worked on the ship, and helped out where I could with the cooking and so on, but in a lot of ways the days there just felt like a rest. A break away from the troubles we'd faced. I didn't see Solomon again in my dreams, and the centred, contented feeling I'd experienced with my lovers stayed with me.

Finally, Tate decreed it time to sail for the town of Nassau, a bit further North in the Bahamian islands.

The ship was packed up and I moved the blankets and pillows back into Tate's room. Zack had claimed my old cabin and settled himself in there. We sailed for most of the day to the port of Nassau.

Tate stood beside me at the prow of the ship as we came in to dock.

"Is it like Tortuga?" I asked.

"Some," he said. "The waters of the harbour are too shallow for a man-o-war, so the Navy tends to stay away. There's no English governor. A little less built up than Tortuga maybe."

I nodded, watching as we pulled into a rickety dock and Anton and James took care of tying the Kelpie up.

"We'll stay at the Mad Parrot tonight, but I'm going to stay with the ship for the first shift," Tate said. "Ezra will go with you and Ora if you want to explore?"

"Yes, I do," I said. "Will there be somewhere to finally get Ora the dress they want?"

And I had that other thing to investigate as well, which Ezra will be none too pleased about, but I need answers about my magic if I can find them, and Sagorika said there are witches in Nassau.

"Indeed," Tate said. "Make sure you get your share off Sagorika."

"Thank you, Tate." I went on my toes to kiss him and then looked around for Ora, who was chatting with Sagorika and Zack. I joined them as the ship bumped gently against the dock.

Sagorika doled out money from the lock box to the crew. The Royal Navy had confiscated our coffers, or at least, the ones they could find. Tate had a secret hiding place somewhere on the ship, and had a certain amount of gold saved up. I couldn't imagine it would last much longer though.

"You'll be wanting your share I expect?" Sagorika asked with a smile.

"Please," I said. I gave Ora a kiss on the cheek and then turned properly to Sagorika.

She dug into the bag at her hip and counted out some coins into my hand.

"Now, if you're looking for a witch," she said. "You want to head to the west and back a few blocks from the shore. Look for the sign of the eye."

I swallowed, my mouth going dry. "Right, yes, of course. Thank you, Sagorika."

Zack shuddered. "You can keep the witches."

Sagorika hip checked him and he stumbled. "Careful, you,

some of the people on this ship - in this conversation - are witches," she said.

"Right, sorry," Zack said. He scrubbed the hair at the back of his head and looked properly embarrassed.

I shook my head and took Ora's arm. "Will we see you two at the Mad Parrot later on?" I asked.

"Absolutely," Sagorika said. "This one's never been to a proper pirate tavern. I expect it'll be even funnier than your first time at the Pickled Oyster, Gid."

I do feel a little like the experienced, senior officer here, which is odd. This is only my second pirate port after all...

"We'll see you tonight, then," I said. Ora and I walked off arm in arm to find Ezra waiting by the gangplank.

He'd made some effort with his appearance again, his hair was extra tall, freshly shaved on the sides of his head and he wore a fresh black shirt and leather trousers.

Although he looked incredible, I didn't envy Ezra those trousers in this heat. I hadn't gone to any particular lengths to look good myself, although I wore a clean white shirt and my nicer pair of trousers from my old life back in Kingston. The only other exception I'd made for the day was to slip a brocade waistcoat on over my shirt, but in pirate style I didn't bother to fasten it.

If Father could only see me now.

Ezra eyed me, something in his eyes telling me he wanted to see me in a leather harness like the last time we'd been at a town, but I shook my head slightly.

"We have chores to do," I said, crisply. "Find a witch, and buy some clothes."

"Of course," Ezra said, sighing. "But perhaps tomorrow we can break out some leather harnesses and such?"

"I'd like that," Ora said, grinning at the both of us. I smiled back.

"Perhaps we can," I said. I gave Ezra a quick kiss on the

cheek and he led the way off the ship on the gangplank. Ours was not the only ship moored here, and all the others looked to be pirate vessels or privateers.

The town of Nassau looked brighter somehow than Tortuga. Perhaps it was less grimy? Or perhaps it was the whitewash used on more of the buildings.

Similar to the other port towns, the main street nearest the port was full of marketplace stalls and people selling their wares. The smell of hot savoury stew, fresh johnnycakes and barbequed lobsters filled the air and set my stomach rumbling.

"I don't understand why humans have to cook absolutely everything," Ora said, pulling a face. "Lobster like that is delicious raw."

"Well, sometimes it's a question of texture," I said.

"Or not getting sick from it," Ezra added. He had one hand resting casually on the hilt of his sword as we walked, and it was as if the crowds parted for us as people saw him. We made our way west, as directed.

"She said a few blocks back from the shore," I said. "To find a witch."

"Surprised there's none here in the market," Ezra said, eyeing a couple of stalls.

"Perhaps they have their own market?" Ora suggested. I shuddered a little, imagining a whole market full of witches.

Even if they aren't in a market there are so many things that could go wrong. What if we inadvertently ask for help from an ally of Solomon's?

Does Solomon even have allies? How far is his reach?

I cleared my throat. "Ora, you can tell if there's magic being done around you, can't you?"

"Yes," Ora said. "Of course."

That made me feel somewhat comforted. At least I wouldn't blindly be going into a witch's den with no protection at all.

As we walked from the bustling main street back into the

town, the road sloped slightly upwards and the crowds thinned. Here, instead of people selling their wares, people lived their lives, doing their ordinary chores or sitting on stoops and watching us go by.

Ezra paid them no attention, just kept on striding forward, his expression inscrutable. Ora's arm was still linked with mine and I took great comfort in their being beside me. The town itself seemed utterly charming, but the task ahead of me was filling my mind with dread.

What if the witch casts a spell over all of us? It won't help that Ora knows it's happening if they're already snagged in it.

I shook my head a little, trying to let such thoughts go, but my stomach was in knots. All hunger had vanished into a solid lump of fear.

"This looks promising," Ezra said. He nodded at a sign painted on the side of a wall. *Magic Alley.*

"Oh, yes, yes it does. Handy, really, that they're willing to signpost it like this."

We paused at the head of the street and looked down it. The buildings were painted or whitewashed the same as the rest of the town, but these doors had signs hung over them with pictures of stars and moons, suns and trees. One had a wave on it, one had a bird.

"How are we meant to choose?" I asked. "I didn't expect there to be so many, I thought..."

Ora squeezed my arm. "Sagorika said the sign with the eye, remember?"

I hadn't remembered. I thanked the Heavens once again that Ora was with me. I took a deep breath. "Thank you, it'd slipped my mind."

"An eye," Ezra said. "There." He started striding towards it, then seemed to remember where we were and his own distaste for the magical arts, and paused, letting us go first.

The door under the sign of the eye was painted purple and

stood ajar. A heavy, cloying scent of incense drifted out from the door and inside seemed to be terribly dark.

Well, time for my etiquette lessons to come in useful again.

I straightened my back and tapped on the door three times before stepping in, letting my arm slip out from Ora's.

"Hello? Excuse me?" I called into the room. Inside the smell was even stronger. It was dark, but light filtered through from behind the blinds on the windows. The room was cluttered with tables, each one holding stacks of books, jars of water and specimens from the ocean. One wall seemed to be lined with tiny jars holding mysterious tinctures of all colours. I wondered what they all did.

"Who's that?" The voice sounded cranky and high, scratchy like a chalk on a slate. I swallowed and stepped further in, comforted at the sound of Ora and Ezra's steps behind me.

"Yes, hello, we just came in on a ship, and I'm looking for some magical help," I said. "Have I - have we come to the right place?"

A shape emerged, stood up, rather, from a chair in the back of the place. A small woman, stooped, wearing a finely laced shawl that looked like spun moonlight over her shoulders. She shuffled forward and straightened up to almost my height, peering into my face.

"Who sent you?"

"Oh, uh, no one. I suppose, Sagorika suggested we find you, but she didn't *send* us exactly," I said. I tried not to flinch back from her gaze, although I wanted to. Something in her gaze was a little too piercing.

"Hmm." The woman didn't look impressed. She looked past me at Ora and then her eyes widened. "Oh, oh, that is interesting."

I glanced over my shoulder, and Ora set down the book they'd picked up and waved their fingers. "Hello there."

"I expect this is the right place for you," the woman said. "I'm

Etta, or Circe, depending on who you ask. What's the difficulty? They stuck as a human or something?"

"I - what?" I asked. "No, we're not here for them, we're here for me."

"You?" She peered into my eyes, her own narrowing. "Well? Why? What's the problem?"

"Etta, it is so lovely to meet you, my name's Gideon," I said, reaching to shake her hand. She eyed my hand and didn't take it.

"Yes, and?"

"And, I have some sort of magic inside me that I don't understand. I was hoping you could uh, do something, a spell or something to find me the source of it, or some way to understand what it is and what it can do."

She stood back and folded her arms, looked me up and down as if she could see right through me. I resisted the urge to shuffle my feet. "Huh. Really?"

"Yes, really," Ezra said, impatiently from behind me. I startled.

"Ezra, please," I said. I shot him a quelling look over my shoulder. I had no idea how that would work, since he was generally the one quelling me, so to speak, but he had to admit I knew what I was doing in this sphere at least.

He folded his arms and sighed.

"Might go better if that one waits outside," Etta said, shaking her head. "He doesn't trust and doesn't believe."

"Oh, I believe all right," Ezra said. "That's the problem."

"I'm sorry," I said. "But I'd be more comfortable if he stayed, if that's all right."

Etta harrumphed and turned away, picking up a black velvet bag. "Sit," she said, and pointed at the row of chairs against the back wall.

I sat down. Ora and Ezra stood side by side, Ezra a few

inches taller, and watched. Ezra distrustfully, Ora with open interest.

Etta pulled a handful of something out of the bag and threw them in the air over the table. They came clattering down onto the table surface, I think they were bones, or small pebbles, and she looked them over.

"Hmm, yes, yes, all right there is more to you than meets the eye." Ora moved up to look over the table as well. They reached a slow hand out to touch one, eyes on Etta, who nodded. "Go ahead siren, touch away."

Ora grinned and started fiddling with the bones.

Etta sat beside me and took my hand in hers, turning it over to examine the palm. "You'd better tell me what has happened, and what it did."

I glanced at Ezra, who looked deeply uncomfortable, his arms folded, watching us closely, but I had begun to trust Etta myself. She gave me a smile when I looked back at her, and I had come here for help after all.

I folded my hands in my lap and began to speak.

I told her what I knew, that my magic spiked inside me during sex, and that the more people involved in the sex, the greater the power within me. I told her how I'd been able to resist Solomon in the dream, although he had no trouble controlling my mind when we were in person - although I had managed to swallow down a truth or two instead of giving it to him. Also that he had seemed to curse me, but I'd been able to get rid of it with Ora and the others.

Although the things I told her were salacious to say the least, she didn't bat an eyelid at my confessions. Finally, I told her about the feeling of being a convergence, and how it seemed to help burn away the curse and she nodded.

"All right, lad, I think I know what could be happening. But to be sure, I'll need some of your blood," she said.

I swallowed hard. "Is it safe?" I asked Ora.

"No?" Ora shrugged.

Ezra bristled and stepped a little closer, his eyebrows drawing together. "Gideon... I'll not have you put yourself in unnecessary danger."

"I need answers," I said.

"And this is the only way." She got up and pulled down a silver bladed knife and a bowl from a high shelf. I swallowed hard, trying to swallow the apprehension making my heart race.

I was afraid, there were things people with magic could do with blood, she could bind me or control me or worse. But I needed answers, and this was the only way, she'd said as much.

Maybe I should try another store on this street?

But Sagorika suggested her.

I have to trust her, I have to get the answer.

I held my arm out to her, pushing the sleeve of my shirt up my arm.

"Good," Etta said. She positioned the bowl underneath, nicked the fleshy part of my forearm with the knife and caught the blood in the bowl.

Ora's eyes were wide, watching and they licked their lips. I quickly looked away. Ezra produced a handkerchief from his trouser pocket and brought it to me. Etta hurried off with the blood, muttering some incantation under her breath.

I took the fabric from Ezra and wrapped it around my arm. "Thank you," I said, but my attention was largely on Etta, watching what she would do.

She pulled down a number of small bottles of various coloured substances off the shelves. She added measured amounts of each to another bowl using a series of variously sized silver spoons with tiny heads and long stems. Finally, she tapped in a little of my blood.

"Interesting, interesting," she murmured. "How about... ohhhh?" She stirred it with a twig and then smiled wide as anything, I could see she was missing a couple of teeth.

I bit my lip so that I could hold back from asking her what she was finding out. She would tell me in her own time, after all.

Perhaps Ezra's training in patience has improved me a little, even in this? Or perhaps I'm too afraid of what the answer might be.

Ezra went back to his position in the middle of the shop, and Ora tried experimentally picking up the bones and throwing them, smiling as they clattered down again.

"These are wonderful," they said. Etta ignored them and continued her work.

Finally, Etta set the bowl down and turned back to me.

"It's in your blood all right," she said. "Inherited. Some generations ago, for it's weak and long been dormant. But you have it there."

"Have what there?" A chill froze my heart. I'd come here for answers but now that I was about to get them I wasn't sure I wanted them at all.

"You've incubus blood," she said, simply.

Ora looked up, their eyes wide.

"Ink-what?" Ezra growled, his patience clearly wearing thin.

"Incubus, not unlike your boy here," she nodded at Ora who frowned.

"I'm not a boy, or an incubus."

"No, but you're not a world away either," she said. She went to the stack of books on the table and pulled one out. The words on the cover read *Types of Fae.*

The title was enough to put a stab of coldness in my heart. Fae?

But Fae were the stuff of myth, legend, long since removed from our world, their influences dwindling to nothing. Surely, she was mistaken.

She opened the book to a page and handed it to me.

.   .   .

I read the passage right through three times, trying to make my mind process what I was reading and make sense of it. It couldn't be true could it?

The hairs on the back of my hair stood up and my breath caught. Creating harems of lovers? I'd done that, although my lovers hardly obeyed my every whim.

The rest of it was too monstrous to contemplate.

"No, this can't be right," I said, slamming the book shut so that I didn't have to look at those hateful words any longer. "There must be some other explanation, I don't... this can't be what I am."

Etta raised an eyebrow at me. "Can it not? Well, maybe I could try a divination with the moon, but it'll cost you."

"What will it cost? I'll pay," I said, shaking my head. I shoved the book away from myself. "You already have to pay for the first spell," she said. "But a moon divination as well? That'll be hrm, five gold pieces."

I swallowed. That seemed like a lot of money. It would be most of what Sagorika had given me, but to find more information, something that showed I wasn't this demon thing she'd found in the book? That would be worth it.

"Yes, of course," I said, standing up. I fumbled the coins out of my pocket and counted them into her hand. "When can you do it?"

She took the gold from me, bit a piece and then slipped it inside her shirt. "If it's clear I can do it tonight," she said. "Come back tomorrow, Gideon. We'll see what we can see."

I swallowed and nodded, standing up. "Thank you, Etta."

"We can go then?" Ezra asked and I nodded. I turned to Ora, who's eyes had narrowed a little and their lips were pursed. I hesitated before holding my hand out to them.

"Come on, Ora, let's go," I said. They took my hand and we all left the witch's store.

Walking into the bright sunlight I had to shield my eyes.

"So, what was all that about then?" Ezra said. "What's the incubus thing she said?"

"It can't be true," I said, briskly. "I don't wish to talk about it."

"That bad, is it?" Ezra said, arching his eyebrow.

"Incubus," Ora said. "She said like me, a bit. Does she mean you might be able to sing like me?"

I thought of the passage I'd read and what I knew of the merfolk. What was the similarity? The killing people? The making people want something?

"I don't know. Not the singing, it didn't say anything about singing. I'm sure she was wrong, anyway."

Ora's mouth twisted to the side and they dropped my hand to put their arm around my shoulders. "You're a maelstrom again, try not to worry too much. She did say it was weak in your blood."

"She said it'd been dormant too," Ezra said. "If it wakes up all the way, does it get to full strength?"

My heart raced, and my temper flared. "Please! There's no point theorising until we have all the information. I'll come back tomorrow, alone, and find out for certain."

Ora's body stiffened against mine and they dropped their arm from my shoulders. I instantly felt awful for snapping at them. It wasn't Ora's fault I didn't like to imagine I had fae blood.

"Sorry," I said, swallowing. "I'm just... I don't want it to be true. It can't be, that's all."

Ora nodded a little and Ezra took a deep breath. "Come on, let's go shopping, didn't you want to buy clothes?"

I shoved all the anger and sadness and fear down inside me and nodded, forcing a smile onto my face. "Yes, clothes shopping. That will be fun."

CHAPTER FIFTEEN - IN WHICH ORA FINALLY GETS SOME OF THEIR OWN CLOTHES

After the stop at the first clothing store, I had relaxed considerably.

There was something about fresh new garments that soothed the soul, and although our main mission was to find something for Ora, I had found a charming silver brocade frock coat that I liked for myself. Ora had tried on a flowing shift not dissimilar to the type Sagorika liked to wear, and I paid for both items.

The next store had partially made shirts that you could have tailored and collect the next day, which Ezra was interested in. He was measured and put a down payment on three black shirts and one for Ora, who liked a pale green fabric they carried, and said they'd like something to go with their skirt.

The next store we found some beautiful things made with locally produced fabrics, lots of large flowers and ocean designs. Ora particularly liked a dress in green and purple with a design of dolphins on it, and I used the last of my coin to buy it for them. I would never have chosen such a thing myself, but Ora looked absolutely perfect when they tried it on.

"There now, you're feeling happier," Ora said as we turned back onto the main market street.

"I am," I said. "Considerably."

The further we'd walked from Magic Alley the surer I felt that Etta had been mistaken. The moon would tell her the truth that night and then I'd go back and find out that perhaps my mother had been a witch or something. Had she been a witch and hidden it somehow? It was unlikely, but not totally unheard of.

Much more likely than fae blood.

Besides, I'd always enjoyed shopping for clothes.

"There's the Mad Parrot," Ezra said, and led the way to the tavern. It appeared to be made of a renovated English villa - there was a generous verandah out front where people were lazing and drinking, and inside I could see more tables in a wide open room.

The upstairs had a long balcony and there were people up there, drinking and laughing as well. There were delicious smells wafting from inside and my stomach rumbled again.

Soon enough, we were settled at a large table on the deck. Tate, Sagorika and Zack joined us, as well as a few others from the crew. Tate ordered a large amount of food and wine for the table, and I was soon forgetting all my cares in the drink.

"How do you like Nassau?" Ezra asked Zack, smirking a little.

"It's very... free?" Zack said.

"You should see Tortuga," Ezra said, shaking his head. "That would blast your socks off."

"What did you do today?" I asked, leaning forward to take Zack's hand and squeeze it, reassuring him.

"Bought some clothes," Zack said, ducking his head. He squeezed my hand back and I thought he was ducking his head to hide his pleased smile.

"We did, too," I said. It warmed my heart to think of Zack

purchasing his own tailored clothing. I knew little of his past, but I had to assume his clothing had all been women's styles before he joined the Navy.

I have helped him find his freedom, I thought, and that feeling warmed my soul.

"Gid, what happened to your arm?" Tate asked, grabbing my arm and turning it so he could see the wound from Etta. "Were you robbed again? I thought Ezra was with you."

"No, I wasn't, he was, it's fine," I said. I tried to tug my hand back but Tate held it fast, frowning. He wanted an explanation. I lowered my voice a little, feeling self-conscious about being overheard. "We went to see a witch, and she needed some of my blood to read what, or, rather, where my magic came from."

Zack's eyes widened. "What did you find out?"

I couldn't meet anyone's eyes. "Nothing yet. She's going to divine overnight and I'm going back tomorrow."

Tate let go of my arm and slipped his hand in mine instead. "You've nothing to worry about, Gid. We love you no matter what."

Gratefully, I leaned against him. There was a sudden lump in my throat and I swallowed it down. It was amazing how much those few simple words could affect me.

"Love you, too," I murmured, hardly trusting myself to speak louder than that.

I took a sip of wine and felt the warm flush of it ease the emotional edge and the lump in my throat loosened.

I looked up to see Ezra looking at me with a peculiar expression. I licked my lips and gave him a smile. He had promised that no amount of magic would stop him caring for me, but if I myself was an entirely magical creature, that was a different story, wasn't it?

He and Ora got along with each other all right, but I knew Ezra was still wary of them.

He winked at me, and picked up a piece of fried chicken and the tension in my chest eased a little.

I looked over to Ora who had pieces of chicken in each hand and was taking bites of first one then the other, looking pleased as punch.

"Where's Zeb?" I asked, turning back to Tate.

"He'll be along later, he was snoozing on the deck when I left. Didn't want to move."

Something stirred in my memory, the dream I'd had of us all settling down in a house somewhere. I didn't know if such a thing was possible, but I wondered... was this the time to bring it up? Probably not. Not when I didn't know what news I'd be sharing with them the next day.

I finished up the food I had on my plate and licked my lips, taking another long drink of wine and sitting back to pat my stomach a little.

Ora sidled closer to me, hands now empty. "Gideon... do you think we could try something new?" Their hand slid onto my thigh and my cock instantly reacted.

New? Yes. I always loved new. What could Ora have in mind?

"Yes, all right."

"Where's our room?" Ora said, turning to Tate.

"Here," Tate dug a key out of his pocket and handed it to Ora. "Room ten."

"Come on, Gideon, we have something to try... Ezra, you could come too, if you like?" Ora raised their eyebrows at Ezra who shrugged and shook his head.

"I might be along later. I'm not done eating."

"Well, can we use some of your supplies?" Ora asked, innocently. My cock stiffened further and I adjusted my trousers, feeling rather exposed. And curious, what could Ora want with Ezra's supplies? What did they have planned?

"I suppose," Ezra said. He smirked and nodded at Tate. "You brought over the sack, did you?"

"Obviously," Tate said, his eyes sparkling. "I'm not a complete idiot, you know."

Ora took my hand and tugged me away, I waved goodbye to the people at the table, my cheeks warming with excitement and anticipation.

CHAPTER SIXTEEN - IN WHICH ORA
AND GIDEON PLAY WITH KNIVES

"Jf I might enquire, what have you got in mind?" I asked Ora. I chuckled as they hurried up the steps, towing me by the hand and I had to speed up so I didn't trip on the steps.

"It's all right if you're not into it, but earlier, the knife and the blood. And I know how much you enjoy pain..." Ora said, a bit vaguely.

My mouth went dry, uncertain if Ora was saying what I thought they might be saying.

"You - you want to cut me?" I asked. We'd got to the top of the stairs and Ora was looking back and forth, trying to match the number on the key to the numbers painted on the door. "It's this one." I tugged them towards the door.

"Well, just a little," Ora said. They fumbled the key into the door and opened it, gestured for me to go first. "I think I could make it really good for you, I mean, I know I can, if you trust me. And I sort of think you'd like to get out of your own thoughts a little, this would do that."

I turned to look at Ora, smiling as the heat from arousal mingled with the warmth of my love for them.

Of course I wanted to be distracted from my thoughts.

"How do you understand me so well?" I asked, softly.

"Right," Ora said. "So you're in?"

I nodded, looked around and spotted Ezra's sugar sack of leather and bondage supplies from Tortuga. "What uh, what gear of Ezra's did you want?"

Ora made sure the door was locked.

"Something to tie you down with," they said. I felt my cheeks warm and heat pool in my stomach. I crouched to rifle through the sack to find my dark brown leather collar, the matching cuffs and some lengths of chain and padlocks. After a moment, I set the collar back inside the sack, because that was mine and Ezra's.

I brought the lot over to Ora who smiled. "Yes, perfect. Now, what else? You have a dagger, don't you?"

"I... yes." I swallowed and unsheathed my dagger and handed it to them, hilt first. My nerves felt on edge, every sense on high alert to Ora now that they had my only weapon.

They didn't bother to carry a blade themselves, because they always had their teeth, a second's tiny bit of shapeshifting magic away.

I'd been afraid of Ora for a while, having seen those teeth and what they could do with them. But I loved and trusted Ora with everything I was. My body was their body, I knew any pain they'd give me would be worth it.

Ora lifted the tip of the blade to my chin and smiled softly. "Do you trust me, Gideon?"

"I do, absolutely," I said, surprised at how quickly I lost my breath, my cock stiffening just as fast.

"Then take your clothes off and get on the bed, handsome." They dropped the blade of my dagger down and I hurriedly tore my shirt off and shucked my trousers, made my way to the bed and lay back on it.

"How do you... how do you want me to lie? On my front or back?" I asked. I sat back up, not wanting to do something that was counterproductive, not when this was the first time Ora and I had done this kind of thing together alone. Of course, Ora had mentioned that things under the sea were somewhat wild, perhaps they'd done something like this before we'd met.

Ora had dropped their own clothing on the floor, they were fussing with the cuffs and the chains as they slowly approached me.

"On your back. Reach for the bars at the top of the bed."

I lay back and raised my arms, tilting my head to look at the headboard, which was a fine carved wooden part of the bed frame, a fence-like railing.

I closed my fingers around two of the bars shoulder width apart and Ora climbed on top of me, their warm skin brushing pleasantly against mine before they settled, straddling my waist and putting their weight on my belly.

Taking their time, they fastened the leather cuffs around my wrists. They bent to kiss me passionately, I lost myself in the kiss, allowing myself to be distracted as they took away my freedom.

They threaded the chains through the metal rings on the cuffs and around the headboard and fastened them with the padlocks.

"There, secure." Ora tilted their head and smiled down at me, looking more predatorial than normal, an anticipatory shiver shot through me. "Can you get away?"

I let go of the bed and tugged against the chains, making them rattle against the rails. I had very little movement. I felt my cock throb in response to knowing this.

My cock and my heart both thrilled, being at the mercy of my lover, letting them do whatever they liked to me and trusting it would bring me a fantastic orgasm at the end... it was desperately exciting.

My skin prickled with desire as I tugged again on the chains

- Ora had been right, I did like pain and I wanted to see how Ora would act, being in charge like this.

"I can't get away," I said, and licked my lips. I relaxed my arms and leaned my head up to try and steal a kiss from Ora. "I'm all yours."

"Mmm." Ora ignored my attempt to kiss them and picked up the dagger again. I dropped my head back to the bed, feeling my heart speed up even more.

"Here's what I think," they said, slowly, their voice a little lower than usual. "I think you should stay very, very still Gideon."

I caught my breath and moaned softly. "Right, yes, good," I said.

With a steady hand and barely any pressure to it, Ora traced the point of the blade down my throat, over my Adam's apple and down to my collarbone.

I barely dared to breathe, I was concentrating so hard on staying still.

The blade traced its way down my skin and the danger of it, the possibility that something could go wrong and the blade could slip had my heart in my throat. I was utterly focused on this one thing, my entire universe distilled down to staring into Ora's eyes and holding as still as I possibly could. It was incredible how much movement I usually had. My chest raising and falling, my fingers moving... I kept it all still.

At some point, Ora would nick my skin with the blade.

They'd said cutting, after all, and I assumed they wanted to taste my blood - they ate blood and flesh - but I had no idea where the cut would occur or when.

"That's it, very good." Ora moved their blade hand away from me, kissed me hard and reached behind them to stroke my cock with their other hand.

I groaned into their mouth, needy and wanting, bucking my hips against their hand and rocking Ora's body up as I moved.

They sat up and tsked a little. "Maybe I ought to chain your legs down too, if you're going to move around like that?"

I groaned, wanting the chains and simultaneously not wanting them to stop the teasing to do it. I shook my head.

"No, sorry, I'll stay still. You don't need to - to bring out more chains."

Ora stroked their hand up the length of me, tugging in a teasing, almost painful way, then turned entirely back to me. This time they leaned over my face, their hands on the arm that Etta had cut into.

They held my arm with one hand and traced the knife around the sore spot, making me hiss through my teeth.

"Tell me if you want me to stop," Ora murmured. I bit down on my lower lip. I didn't want them to stop. It hurt, well, stung really, but I wanted to see where Ora and the dagger would take me.

And I couldn't deny that the excitement and the danger of it was arousing.

"I want more," I said, my voice hoarse. "Please, do it."

Ora smiled and kissed me so softly on the lips that I was afraid they were going to stop altogether, but then they pressed their forehead to mine.

"I know you do, I can taste it," Ora said. "You're... you're afraid there's darkness within you. That the magic inside is evil and will consume you."

I swallowed hard, surprised more than anything. Ora's words were true but they'd seemed to come out of nowhere. They straightened up and looked me in the eye.

"Isn't that right? The witch said the thing you were, it wasn't so different to me."

"I..." I couldn't lie to Ora, no matter how much I wanted to, just as I couldn't lie to myself. "Yes. I'm afraid that's true."

"But darkness isn't necessarily a bad thing," Ora said. They dragged the point of the blade into the wound and I hissed. The pain shot sparks of white hot light through my arm and down into my chest, where my body promptly turned it into need and delectable warmth, streaming down into my cock and tightening my balls.

Although I wanted to squirm under them, thrust into the air and tug my arm away from Ora's grip, I stayed completely still.

Ora leaned down and licked at the wound.

I allowed a little movement, I turned my head to watch. The cut had begun to bleed again and Ora caught each droplet on their tongue. It was strangely fascinating to watch. I had thought I'd already done the most intimate possible things with Ora, but this seemed even more private and intimate again.

My life blood inside them. I want them to do this while they fuck me... I want more.

I moaned and Ora sat up, licking their lips. "You like it?"

"Yes," I groaned. "Please, do more, I want more, more cutting. Taste me, please. Fuck me, I need it."

Ora moved the knife to my other arm and quickly made a slice across the skin there. It was so fast it barely hurt while it was happening. The pain came afterwards in a wave of sharpness, which went straight to my cock.

Ora wrapped their hand around my arm just below the cut and squeezed, letting the blood ooze out a little before they licked it up.

I moaned and rolled my hips very gently. "Please, I need you to touch me, Ora."

"You do? Well then..." Ora sat up and reached behind to stroke my cock and hummed a moment. They shifted off my middle and between my legs, pushing them apart. They reached down to stroke themselves, and I watched, panting hard. "Oh yes, you're ready for me."

Ora's natural self-lubrication had kicked in and their hand came away slick from their own cock and they teased me, stretching me with their fingers.

"Ora, yes, yes please," I breathed, turned my head to look at the knife cut in my arm and bit my lip. I loved it.

"Patience, love," Ora chuckled. "I've got you... I'm here. Just relax"

"You're starting to sound like Ezra," I groaned. "Talking about patience."

Ora laughed at that, all of the threatening, controlling, dagger-wielding aura vanished for a moment. Ora pushed inside me, and I groaned with the feel of them stretching me, that incredible drag and sting. I shifted, moving my legs further apart and pushing against them.

Ora brought the dagger up again and pressed the point of the blade into my chest on the left, just above my nipple and I went still again, hardly daring to breathe with the blade so close to my heart.

They met my gaze and the intimidating smoulder came back into their expression. There was a question there as well.

"Yes," I breathed. "Do it."

Ora tilted the dagger and scratched a line across my skin. Once again the pain sent sparks through me that quickly elevated to something incredible. I felt the fire inside me building, the magic?

"I feel something," I gasped. Ora dipped a finger into a drop of my blood and sucked it off. I bit my lip and watched their face, seeing the inhuman cut of their cheekbones, the slight shimmer to their skin that betrayed the merfolk nature of them if you knew to look for it.

They were absolutely stunning to observe, and my cock throbbed with need. They pulled most of the way out of me and then slowly pushed back in, dipped their finger in my blood again and then offered it to me, their finger inches from my mouth.

I could take it, if I wanted. I inhaled, smelling the iron tang.

I felt on the edge of something. And that something was a

point of no return. I hesitated although my mouth watered to taste it.

"Don't be afraid," Ora said, softly, their eyes piercing. I dropped my eyes from theirs to the finger, to the red drop of blood on the tip of it. "Whatever is inside you, whatever that witch finds, I love you, and I'll stay with you as long as you want me to."

I swallowed, leaned forward and licked their finger, groaning at the sharp, iron taste of the blood, and then sucking their finger into my mouth and rolling my tongue around it.

Ora groaned and their eyes closed, so I nibbled their finger a little.

"You don't seem afraid at all, now," Ora said, pulling their finger out of my mouth and rocking their hips again.

"What I read in that book," I said, groaning as they started to rock their hips more again. "That's what scared me. That I might be some kind of... sex demon."

"I don't think you are," Ora said. "It sounded like it's just a bit of fae blood, a few generations back."

It felt strange to be talking so deeply while we fucked, but at the same time we were both there in the moment. I wanted to open my soul to Ora as much as I could, and I wanted them to cut me again, but that could come later.

"If it's true, that I have incubus blood, then... then I've taken advantage of all of you," I said. My voice cracked at that, finally.

Ora set the dagger down and slipped their hand behind my neck, wrapped their other one around my body. "I don't think that's possible."

"It could be, if it's magic making me attractive to you, making you want to do all these things with me. And worse, that because you're doing them with me I'm feeding off you and killing you all...."

Ora shook their head and kissed me deeply. Finally breaking

it when we were both breathless. "You're not killing us. And I choose you, Gideon. I'd choose you over and over."

I inhaled deeply and nipped at their jaw, now that I'd expressed my absolute worst fears over the text in the book, I felt a little more relaxed, a little freer. Ironic really.

I tugged against the chains on my wrists, exulting in the restriction I felt.

"Now fuck me, please Ora."

Ora held me tight and started thrusting, kissing at my jaw and neck, making me moan and squirm and yank on the chains as if I could somehow break through them and hold Ora, push them deeper inside me. It didn't work.

Ora let go of my waist to push their hand between us to stroke my cock. I held back on my orgasm although it was imminent.

"Come with me, love," Ora murmured. They nipped at my throat as I nodded.

After a few more thrusts we were both reaching completion, without words Ora told me to let go and I did, bucking into their hand as they filled me with their seed.

My arms yanked against the chains again and I cried out, feeling the cuts on my body as my muscles spasmed and relaxed again.

We slowly came to a rest, and Ora pulled out and stroked me a couple more times before settling beside me and unlocking the padlocks.

The moment my arms were free, I threw them around Ora and pulled them close, pressing my head into their chest and inhaling the scent of them.

Ora held me close and stroked my hair.

"You were so good," Ora said. "I'm really proud of you."

I felt my body shudder with an emotion I couldn't name, or possibly a storm of emotions. But it didn't feel bad, particularly. I felt like I might cry, or laugh, or both at the same time.

"It's all right, love," Ora said. "I love you, and whatever happens, we'll still be together."

They held me, stroked my back and reassured me until I came back to myself, feeling refreshed in a way, the release had been more than physical.

CHAPTER SEVENTEEN - IN WHICH THE TRUTH IS DISCOVERED AND SHARED

It wasn't too long after we'd settled into the bed that Tate, Zeb and Ezra came knocking on the room door. We had the key, so Ora got up to let them in.

They were all a little warm from alcohol and although Ezra excused himself to the private room next door, he gave me a warm kiss before saying goodnight. He also eyed the cut marks on my body and nodded approvingly.

"All right, I'd like to be a part of that next time."

"Fine with me," I said. I felt weary and happy, and over anything else, I felt indulgent.

He went next door.

Tate and Zeb pulled their clothes off and piled into the bed with Ora and I, and we fell asleep cuddling and tangling our limbs together in a big warm pile.

In the morning, I got up and pulled my clothes on, extracting myself from under Tate's arm. Ora got up too and without speaking we slipped out of the room together and went downstairs.

"Are you sure you want to go back to the witch alone?" Ora asked.

I'm not, honestly. I don't want to go back at all, I don't want the answer to be something I don't like. I don't want to sit there alone and hear whatever she has to say.

I want Ora to hold me and tell me everything will be all right again. I want nothing to change.

But all of that is cowardly, isn't it? I don't want to be a coward.

"No, I'm not sure," I said. "But I think it's something I have to do on my own. I need to find out and learn what I can."

"All right." Ora kissed my cheek. "I'm going for a swim in the harbour then."

I watched them walk towards the dock and then I turned up the street.

It was early in the morning still, and a lot of the stalls weren't operating yet. There was a man making johnnycakes on a hot griddle and I stopped to buy one to fortify myself for whatever news Etta had.

I ate it as I walked up the streets, stepping around a man snoring on the cobblestones, and avoiding a particularly angry looking rooster roaming the road. My steps slowed the closer I got to Magic Alley, but I got there in the end.

I walked up Magic Alley to Etta's. As with the market road, the stores here didn't seem to be open yet, and Etta's door was closed. But I didn't want to come back later, so I stepped up to it and rapped on it three times.

If she didn't open up, I'd just wait on the stoop until she did. I didn't think I'd be able to force myself to come back to the store if I went back to the inn now.

For several long minutes, I didn't hear anything, but then there was movement inside and at the same time my heart leapt and my stomach sank.

Etta opened the door, she was wearing a purple robe, tied at the waist but her hair was freshly brushed.

"Ah yes, I thought you'd be in early," she said. "Come on, then. Alone today are you?"

"Yes," I said. She held the door open for me and I went inside.

"Come on, sit, have some tea," she said. She seemed to have been expecting me in truth, because there was a teapot on the table where she'd cast the bones the day before and two teacups.

She nodded for me to sit and I did, gratefully. Now that the moment of truth was imminent my knees had started to feel weak.

She poured the tea and pushed a teacup towards me, then sat down opposite. I sniffed the tea, it smelled delicious, herbal and flowery, and it made my mouth water. It also flooded me with comfort.

"Now, dear," she said. "I know you were hoping for something new, but I don't have any other answers for you."

My heart sank and I sighed, looking into the teacup. In some way, I'd known that she'd hit on it the day before.

"Before you pitch yourself into despair, though," she said, not quite scolding but with a sharp edge to her voice. I looked up at her. "Because I suspect that part of what you've inherited is that you'll have very intense emotions, ones that could consume you. But I want to show you a little more of what's known about incubus and succubus."

I took a deep breath and set the teacup down. I felt volatile, as if I might crush the china if I held it in my hand much longer.

"Right, all right," I said. "Please, tell me."

"Well, for a start," she said. "The moon tells me you have a lot of empathy."

"The moon... talked to you? About me?" I asked. I was glad I'd put the cup down for I surely would have dropped it at that.

Etta rolled her eyes and cleared her throat. "Yes, now *listen*. She said you have the ability to feel a lot of things that aren't just yours, that belong to others as well, and if you want someone to feel something, you can give them a push and that will happen."

"A push?"

"Mmhm, I expect lately, from what you told me yesterday, it's been attraction, sexual desire."

I sat back in my chair and thought hard. "The officer, uh, Carrol, on the Trinity Royal," I said. "He... I made him want me, even though I didn't want him like that, I used it to get information out of him."

She nodded and sipped her tea. "Just so. It'll be something you can use. More than that, when you understand more about what you can do, it becomes a strength. And when you have your strength, you can protect the ones you love."

I can what?

"I don't understand," I said. My heart was racing now. Etta turned and pulled a book onto the table, she opened it to a bookmarked page.

"Most of the lore we have on fae kind is lost, and the fae... well, aside from your friend and their kind, most of them don't come to our world any more. But the stories are still around."

"I know some of those stories," I said. I remembered Mother reading them to me, telling stories from when she'd been a girl. Misery seeped into my voice and made my heart heavy. "The stories say they used to enchant humans, make them do all sorts of horrid things. Steal their children, steal them away for what felt like a day but was actually a hundred years."

Etta reached her hand out and covered mine with it. I looked into her eyes and there was a hardness there. "You're not full fae," she said. "You're still human, and in fact, mostly human. But I think you've... you've woken up some of the fae magic inside you."

"You can't possibly - Do you mean, through sex?" I asked, half laughing.

"Exactly. The more you have, the more magic takes notice, the more your blood remembers its birthright."

I shook my head and laughed again. "I don't understand, does this mean my parents have fae blood too?"

"Very unlikely they both do. Most likely it's been handed down on one side of the family only. Moon didn't tell me that."

I bit my lower lip. "I have no idea about my heritage, really. My parents sailed from London when I was a child and I only ever knew them not my grandparents. Mother died when I was young... And Father...well, it can't possibly be from Father."

Etta shrugged one shoulder.

"Whoever it was would be someone charming, someone who people want to be around, someone who lights up a room," Etta said. Her smile was sad and she pulled her hand back from mine, pushed my tea towards me instead.

I thought for a moment on what I remembered of my mother, how she'd made my father so happy, how the loss of her had stolen the joy from his life. All my memories tinged with the incredible joy and love I felt around her.

Yes, that made sense.

I could ponder that another time though, Right now, I needed more information only Etta could give me.

"What did you say about protection, before?" The book had said that terrifying thing about gathering harems and feeding off their energy, but protection only sounded good.

Etta shrugged. "The moon told me, when you have your strength you can protect the ones you love. She doesn't get more detailed than that. But I did think... here, this might help you."

She pulled out a small drawstring bag from her pocket and set it in front of me. I eyed it. The bag was black with a moon painted on it, and whatever it held looked solid. Like a box perhaps.

"What's that?"

"Cards," she said. "Oracles. Your merfolk may be able to read them, or you can yourself. Give you some direction when you need it."

I picked up the bag and opened the string. Inside were a deck of cards, but when I pulled them out they weren't ordinary playing cards, they were painted with strange images on the fronts of them.

The first one I looked at showed a person in a garden blooming with tropical flowers. They had large coins all around their feet, each coin had a star on it. I turned it to show Etta.

"Good fortune that one, prosperity, see the coins? That's money. Hard work, to build the garden, to make it look good. But hard work pays off. You see?"

I bit my lip and looked at it again. Now that I had touched them I wanted the cards very badly. "You're giving these to me?"

Etta snorted. "Selling them, pretty. Selling."

I pulled out my coin purse but it was very light. "I don't have much coin at the moment."

"Blood," she said, bluntly. "Give me some more of that blood and we'll call it square."

I hesitated for just a moment. "All right." I shuffled through the cards as she rose to get her knife and bowl again. The images were absolutely breathtaking - stars, people, cups, wands, swords. I came upon a card with a stone tower, struck by lightning. It gave me a chill feeling.

"What does this one mean?"

Etta came back to the table and set the bowl down, snorted again. "What would your guess be?"

I looked at the tower again. It was being destroyed. "Destruction, uh, maybe ruin?"

"Change," she said. She gestured for my arm and I held it out, setting the cards back into their bag so they'd be out of the way. "The kind of change that breaks things, but new things come from it. Might look bad, might feel bad, but it's not bad in and of itself. Change brings promise of the future, don't you think? You can rebuild something from destruction." With that, she raised her knife.

I braced myself but it still hurt like the dickens when Etta sliced her knife through my flesh. She had none of the precision of Ora, or perhaps she did but didn't care as much about how it felt to me.

I hissed as she turned my arm, squeezed it and let a generous amount of blood drip into the bowl.

"Change isn't always bad," I said, through my teeth. "I suppose I understand that."

She held my arm over the bowl longer than I would have liked, but when I tugged against her grip she dug her fingernails in. Finally she let me go and offered me a scrap of muslin to press against the cut.

Feeling a little resentful, I nursed the wound. "What are you going to do with my blood, anyway?"

She shrugged. "Some spells, some tinctures, might sell a bit, I don't know. Not your problem now, is it?"

My stomach sank. I hoped there wasn't anything injurious she could do to me with my blood, but I suspected there was.

The old stories, the warnings. Names held power, and blood held more... But she was right, it was too late now. I've given it freely to her.

Sighing a little, I stood up and pocketed the bag of cards.

"Thank you for all your help, and for asking the moon and everything," I said.

Etta nodded. "Think on it, pretty boy. Don't do anything rash or foolish, and pay attention to what you're feeling."

"Right, yes, of course, thank you" I said. I hastily fled her store.

This time as I exited the shop I felt another whirlwind of conflicting emotions.

Pay attention to what you're feeling, she'd said.

Oh, Mother, what have you given me?

I cast my eyes up to the sky, and saw the moon just dropping towards the horizon, a pale disc in the morning sunlight. I silently thanked the moon, and then walked back down to the market road.

I was feeling... I was afraid. I could well have been affecting all of my lovers with my magic without even realising I was doing it. That made me feel sick to the stomach, the idea that I could have coerced them into wanting me. I felt dirty.

And then the greater danger, that them being around me - and loving me - was allowing me to somehow feed off them, drain their emotions and their lives with it.

When I reached the dock, instead of turning left towards the Mad Parrot, I turned right and kept walking.

I had to tell my lovers the truth, and let them know there's a chance I could have influenced them, find out what they had to say about it. And then we'd... we'd work something out between us from there.

Some part of me was elated though, under all the worry and fear. There was a part of me that sang the truth of it, and rejoiced in being known.

I let myself stand a little taller as I walked, straightening my back not because my etiquette teacher had coached me to, but because I understood something about myself. I had power now, and I could learn how to use it, what it was good for.

Better, I could use it to protect the ones I love. I could be more useful than I had been previously... perhaps I could protect them from Solomon's influence?

It did seem that I was able to eject him from my dreams, perhaps my presence would work like a shield to keep him away in future?

And I had the cards, which... I wasn't sure how much I'd be able to read from them, but the pictures seemed quite intuitive. Perhaps Ora would have seen something similar before and could help?

Part of me told me to run away and never look back - that my lovers would all be better off without me and I should just take passage on the first ship leaving the dock. Although it was tempting, I had run away from my problems before, that's how I found Tate and the Grey Kelpie, after all.

But I was too selfish by half. I couldn't stand the thought of going to sleep without Tate and Zeb, or of never seeing Ora again, or never knowing what Ezra had in store for me next. After being alone in the infirmary on the Trinity Royal I never wanted to be alone again.

Even if it was what was best for them, I couldn't leave them.

I sighed, stopped walking and looked out at the harbour. Counted the ships, found the Grey Kelpie and rested my eyes there. For better or worse, that was my home now and I couldn't run away from it.

I'd just have to go back to the Mad Parrot and tell them all what I knew, and what I was afraid of.

The cards were a comforting weight in my hand.

Just have to go back there and face the consequences, whatever they are. Honesty is so important, and I want all of my lovers to know the full truth.

I turned back towards the Mad Parrot, walking slowly. There were a few more people around now, a few more stalls in the market.

As I got closer to the tavern a woman approached me, her face bright and smiling.

"Hello, love," she said. "Looking for some company?"

"Uh, no, not really," I said, giving her a polite smile.

"Aw, don't be shy now, where's that accent from? Sounds very posh..."

She moved to block my way. I took another look at her. She wore a loose shirt and a long skirt that had a rip or split up the side, showing off a lot of leg.

Oh, yes, right, a doxy.

"Oh, I uh, I think you have the wrong idea," I said. "I'm not uh, I'm not interested in women."

"Hm, prude," she said, folding her arms over her ample chest.

"No, no, I'm really not, not that," I said. "I just uh, prefer the company of men, that's all."

She snorted and I side stepped to walk past her.

"Wait a moment," she said, and I stopped, level with her, and glanced at her. She looked past me and shook her head. "Never mind."

I turned to see Ora approaching, their hair wet, wearing a shirt that clung to their damp chest and a pair of similarly damp trousers. They looked cheerful enough to me, but if you didn't know them I suspected they looked utterly feral.

"Morning Ora!"

The doxy went back to her alleyway and Ora gave me a kiss hello.

"How'd it go?" They asked. "I saw you staring out to sea and thought I'd better come back in."

I shrugged. "Well, you know, I'm a maelstrom. But I want to talk to everyone about it."

Ora slipped their arm through mine and we started walking. "Very sensible," Ora said, patting my hand where it held their arm.

The inn was in sight now, which was a comfort. I had heard rumours back in Kingston of doxies being used as lures for pickpockets or similar, although I had no solid evidence the doxy had anything bad in mind for me.

The tavern tables were busy, a lot of people seemed to have slept at the tables or on benches, or just on the patch of scrubby grass in front of the verandah.

I couldn't see any sign of any of my lovers at the tables so I led

Ora upstairs and knocked on the door of room ten. And then room nine because I presumed that was where Ezra was staying.

Room nine's door opened and Ezra looked out, his hair mussed from sleeping and wearing only his trousers. My heart and my cock responded positively to seeing him like that, all soft and undone, his chest bare.

"Gideon, Ora, you all right?" He asked, and then yawned.

"Yes, just, would you mind terribly coming next door? I want to talk to you all about what the witch said," I said. Ezra nodded and pocketed his key, closing his door as he walked out into the hall.

Room ten's door opened and Tate gestured us in. He looked a bit fresher, as if he'd been in the process of getting up when I'd knocked. Ora and Tate kissed each other hello and then went into the room, I followed with Ezra behind me.

I felt hands on my hips, pulling me to a stop, and turned to see Ezra looking expectant.

"Good morning," he said.

"Good morning."

"Where's my kiss?" Ezra said. "I'm used to them now." Then he leaned in to kiss me. I kissed him back, a little surprised, and smiled. I flushed warm and happy at those words and the kiss. Ezra was getting sweeter by the day.

Or possibly it was something to do with my magic and him getting accustomed to a certain amount of connection to me? Was that something that could happen?

Inside the room, I purposefully pulled a chair into the centre so that I could sit where I wasn't touching anyone - the absolute counter to what I felt like doing. But I had to remain separate, I didn't know how they'd react to me. I wanted more than anything to lean against Tate, to feel his warm strength. Or to have Zeb sprawl over my lap and calm my nerves. Anything. But no. Not now. I had to tell them what I knew first.

Ezra leaned against the wall nearby, folding his arms. Tate and Zeb settled on the bed, both of them looking at me expectantly.

Ora took my hand and went to sit on the floor beside me but I shook my head.

"Not - not right now," I said. "I want you all to hear this before... before you react however you choose to react."

Ora squeezed my hand, dropped it and settled on the bed on the other side of Tate to Zeb.

Ezra shifted a little, I heard him huff out his breath. I thought, out of all of them, Ezra was likely to have the biggest problem with what I was about to tell them.

Tate nodded at me. "Go on, Gideon, we're all listening."

"Right, so, you know, I went to the witch to ask about... about the magic inside me," I said. "Which, you've all felt, so. That's not news." I shook my head. I didn't want to tell them. I was resisting, stalling for time, and I shouldn't. I licked my lips and started telling them what I knew.

I told them I had fae blood, that the particular type of fae was incubus, and about the sex magic, and the way it had awakened - because of all of them.

I found myself looking at my hands as I spoke, twisting my fingers together. My heart was so afraid that they'd be looking at me with disgust, or worse, fear.

I cleared my throat and looked up, forced myself to face their reactions. None of them looked afraid, a little surprised perhaps, and Ezra's eyebrows had drawn together as if there were a puzzle he had to solve, but no disgust.

Well, I hadn't told them the worst parts, better do that.

"She said, Etta said that incubus are naturally charming, more than charming. Magically magnetic. That they can, uh, I can lure people in I suppose. That they gather groups of lovers who become dedicated to them, and they... then they..." I trailed off. Cleared my throat and forced myself to keep speaking.

"They feed on the emotions of those lovers until they're, well. Used up, um. Dead. That I... there's a chance I could be feeding off your emotions and, somehow, draining your life essence."

Tate's head tilted to the side. "But you're not actually fae, isn't that right?"

"Right," I said, confident on that front. "She thought the fae blood was a few generations back in my line. On my mother's side, I think. She's a lot more charming than Father."

"So, the likelihood that you could actually drink our emotions seems... low," Tate said. He frowned. "Right?"

I shrugged helplessly. "She said I'd activated the blood, and the more I did... The more sex I have, the more strength the magic will have. I don't know what it means."

"You're not feeding on us," Ora said, with certainty. "I'd feel it if you did."

Ezra looked at Ora and cleared his throat. "How sure are you?"

I felt a pang stab through my chest - Ezra was afraid. Or at least, wary of me. And I couldn't blame him at all. But it still hurt.

"Sure," Ora said. "I'd feel it. I can feel magic, and I can tell what Gideon is feeling sometimes. It would be obvious to me. He hasn't. If anything, I think you've amplified our emotions so that we can all feel them, especially during sex."

Oh Mother, I hope you're not listening to this. What a conversation. What a change from the life I led a few months back.

"Well then, we have an early warning. Ora can let us know if they sense anything new like that," Ezra said. "Nothing to worry about."

"Unless it happens," I said, miserably. "Then what?"

"We deal with it when it happens, *if* it happens, which I don't think it will." Tate said. He gave me an encouraging smile. "You're still mostly human, Gid."

"Mostly being the essential word there," I said, lifting a

finger. "And… I'm worried it means that I've somehow influenced you all into being my lovers when you may not have wanted to be. That I've… I don't know, compelled you all. Enchanted and overcome your natural inclinations somehow." I breathed out heavily, looking between them a bit more desperately now.

"You didn't coerce me," Tate said, flatly, without hesitation. "*I* seduced *you*, if I recall correctly."

"Same here," Ezra said. "Besides…" He tapped his finger against his chin, right where his neatly trimmed goatee was. "Didn't you say you somehow woke the magic within you by taking lovers? How could your magic have worked on us before you'd awoken it?"

"I… Oh," I said. I shifted in my seat, thinking that through. "Right, I hadn't considered… but even having the blood, she said, makes you more charming."

"You're cute, but you're hardly irresistible," Tate said. He gave me a warm smile. "I think Ezra and I, we were in our right minds when we decided to seduce you."

"It didn't affect me at all," Ora said. "I'd have sensed it in you. Instead our souls knew each other, it's a totally different thing."

I caught my breath and gazed into Ora's eyes.

Ora wouldn't lie about this. I'm not entirely sure Ora knows how to lie.

I looked at Zeb, finally, who shrugged. "I picked you before any of the rest did, Gid, don't you remember?"

"You were a cat then."

"I still picked you."

I rubbed my hand over my face, hardly able to believe what I was hearing from them all. "None of you seem as concerned about this as you should be."

I felt a hand on my shoulder, warm and reassuring. I looked up to see Ora, smiling down at me. "We're aware now, but…

honestly, I think you're making this more of a problem than it has to be."

"It seems like a pretty big problem!" I exclaimed.

Tate laughed, but it wasn't an unkind laugh. "Gideon, you wouldn't be you unless you were worrying, but in this case I think Ora's right. We know the possible risks, you have your answers about the power inside you, and it can't all be bad, right?"

Zeb shifted into cat form and jumped into my lap, kneading at my legs and purring, reassuring me the best way he knew how. Smiling, I petted his silky black fur.

But I didn't say anything more until I knew what Ezra had to say. I looked at him. He met my gaze and for a moment his expression remained blank. Then his face split into a wolfish smile that never ceased to make my heart speed up.

"Gideon, you're the best damn pet I've ever taken, I'm not going to give you up. Besides I'm used to having all of these lovers to choose from." He gestured at the others.

A weight lifted off my shoulders and I smiled then, sighing out my breath.

"Oh thank the lord, I didn't expect... I actually considered just running away when I found out but I realised I couldn't give up any of you," I said.

Tate got up and crossed the room, Ezra a few steps behind him. I scooped Zeb into my arms and the rest of my lovers closed around me.

It was something I'd never experienced before. Although I'd hugged each of them, I'd never hugged all of them at once. In truth it was more like they wrapped their bodies around me in a protective circle.

The magic inside me swelled up into a warm golden light that felt like it was radiating out of my skin. Being surrounded by them all in such a way, being enclosed in their love and acceptance was almost as powerful as when we all made love together.

I felt tears leaking out, tears of joy and gratitude and an overwhelming love for each and every one of them.

"Thank you," I said, against Ora's shoulder. "Thank you."

Tate squeezed Ora and Ezra closer against me and I chuckled, feeling slightly squashed but in a good way. Zeb mewed softly in my arms and shoved his head against my neck.

Finally they broke away and Tate suggested we head downstairs for breakfast.

CHAPTER EIGHTEEN - IN WHICH THE FUTURE IS CONSIDERED

We had a tasty meal at the tavern, then Ezra, Ora and I headed back to the tailor's to pick up the clothing we'd had fitted the day before. We also went to the post office so Ezra could check if there was any mail for him.

"Who'd be sending mail for you?" I asked, but Ezra shook his head.

"I'll tell you another day. Today we've had quite enough revelations."

The mystery tugged at me a little, until I saw a stack of leather bound notebooks with blank pages. They seemed to be calling my name, somehow. I used the last of my coin to buy two of them, in burnished red leather, and a pen and inkwell to use with them. Perhaps I could start recording my thoughts, or the particularly strange parts of my adventure.

Perhaps I could write my own romance novel?

From midday Zeb, Ora and I took a shift on the ship, keeping watch and relieving James and Anton to go enjoy Nassau.

When Shem and Zack came to relieve us, we made our way back to the Mad Parrot and joined Tate and Ezra at a table on the verandah. There were several platters of fried chicken, plantains and breads, as well as beans and some other vegetables.

They had one glass of beer each and a map unfolded in front of them. I slid into a seat opposite Tate and started piling my plate with food.

"What's going on?" I asked.

Ora sat beside me and Zeb took the seat next to Ezra, reaching for the plate of chicken and pulling it towards him.

"We're trying to decide what to do after Nassau," Ezra said, taking a drink of his beer.

"Why can't we stay here?" Ora asked. "It's nice. And there's a whole street full of witches."

"It's not safe to stay anywhere for too long," Tate said. "Not while Gideon's father and Solomon are both looking for us so tirelessly."

I looked down at my plate, feeling like I'd betrayed everyone again. "I don't know how to call him off," I said.

"No one expects you to," Ezra said. He met my gaze and winked at me.

My stomach turned over with guilt all the same.

Perhaps I can't control him, or call him off, but it remains my fault that he's ordered the British Navy to chase us.

And they know the name of the ship, and there's surely only a matter of time before they find us again. Tate's right, Nassau is far too obvious a place for us to remain.

"Besides all that, we don't know if anyone here in Nassau recognises us, and there is a bounty out, and someone might be sending our whereabouts to the Navy," Tate said. "It's just… it's safer not to stay still for too long."

"What other options do we have?" Zeb asked. "Back to Tortuga?"

Tate shook his head. "We can't go anywhere they'd expect, and that definitely counts as expected. People know us there, people who may've been paid coin for information."

"Which leaves us with England, which seems foolhardy, so much sailing; Singapore, which... well, it's a gamble; or the New World, which is probably the last place they'd look and therefore the obvious choice, to me," Ezra said.

"Or Havana," Tate said. He looked at the map and tapped it with his index finger, drumming an impatient beat. "Maybe Taipei, there's a lot of options. And I don't know, but I feel like we're running away again."

"What's our other option, Captain?" Ezra said, putting some grit into the word captain. "Fight off the entire Royal fleet on our own? Get captured again and taken to the gallows?"

"No, of course I don't mean that, but maybe if we had some way to get to Solomon, he'd stop assisting them to communicate so fast." Tate sighed, snagged a piece of chicken off the plate Ora was working his way through.

"I think there were other witches involved," I said, hesitantly. "I can't be sure, but I think they said witches, plural to me. Not witch."

Tate and Ezra both blinked at me and Ezra shook his head, laughing mirthlessly. "We can't fight Solomon, we tried and he almost killed us all. If Ora hadn't been there with their magic song, we'd have drowned, and he'd have gutted you like a fish."

Both of them were getting angrier, it was obvious from the tension in their voices but in their body language as well. Ora glanced at me and slipped their hand in mine.

"I could sing again," Ora said. "Hold Solomon off for a time, give you an opening."

"He'd see us coming leagues away," Ezra said. "It's not an option."

My stomach turned over unpleasantly and I realised I was tearing a bread roll into small pieces. I hated to see them quarrel like this, but I had no idea how to help.

"Then what? I'd like to hear your solution," Tate said, his voice getting louder. He took a deep drink of beer.

"I think we should fight, too," Zeb said. "We took care of the men who were on the Kelpie easy enough. We can outwit them."

"If we want to save our hides, our best bet is to go somewhere they won't think we would go and lay low," Ezra leaned forward and slapped his palm on the map, making us all jump.

"Like a coward. Like we're frightened and can't bear to face up to anything," Tate spat.

"I'm not afraid, *Captain*, I'm being sensible. They were very ready to string us both up, and I don't fancy our chances if they catch us again. Solomon or not, we'll be dancing from the yardarm of the first ship that catches us."

Tate's face went red. He couldn't deny that. Our escape would have humiliated Captain Thornton and the entire British Navy. If another ship was to catch the Kelpie, they wouldn't take the risk of us escaping again.

Tate huffed and folded his arms, glaring at Ezra. "Maybe we should go to India, and hide with your wife."

My heart seemed to stop for a moment.

Wife? Did he really just say that Ezra had a wife? That couldn't be.

Ezra stood up so fast and so violently his chair fell backwards, making a loud crash. His eyes narrowed and his voice went very low. "How dare you bring her up!"

Tate shrugged, a nasty smile on his face. "Nice big place she has there, isn't it? Could hide us all. Of course, you'd have to face up to -"

Ezra had pulled a blade out from his hip holster and was holding it with a shaking hand, pointing it at Tate.

Ora stood up, starting to hum.

There are too many people around, I thought wildly, looking around us and getting to my feet, too. *If Ora sings it will alert everyone to what they are, and if Tate's right and people have been talking about us, for all we know we've just blown whatever cover we could have had.*

I raced around the table to take hold of Ezra's arm. I couldn't hold him back, he was much stronger than I am, but I could maybe remind him not to attack Tate.

Neither Ezra or Tate had moved, they were at an impasse, staring at each other. It was almost as if I could sense lightning passing back and forth between them. The power of their anger, and their blasted stubbornness.

"Stop, Ezra, please," I said, tugging on his hand. Catching what I was trying to do, Ora went to Tate's side, and put their hand on his shoulder. "Neither of you mean this, I'm sure. Just... try and relax. Try to calm down, and for God's sake put away the knife."

Ezra broke the stare to look at me, his expression still thunderous. But as he met my eyes I saw pain in them, an unspeakable sadness I'd never expected to see there.

"I'm calm."

Slowly, he put the knife away. He gave Tate another glance, pulled his arm out of my grasp and turned on his heel, stalking away into the night.

Ora was murmuring to Tate, who seemed to be at least a little calmer.

I swallowed, turning to watch Ezra go and chewing my lip. Perhaps I ought to go after him? I hated the thought of him out there alone, fuming with anger.

It wasn't that he couldn't look after himself, of course he could, but whatever Tate had meant with that quip about a wife, it had hit Ezra hard.

"Will he..." I asked, turning back to Tate. Tate had known Ezra the longest, after all. Tate shook his head.

"He'll be fine, Gid. I shouldn't have said that, I was out of line. He'll walk it off and be back in the morning. I'll apologise to him, we can make a plan for the future tomorrow."

He sighed mightily and picked up his glass of ale, eyed it and then downed the rest in one.

My stomach turned over and then again. It was like that morning all over again, worrying that Ezra and the others would reject me for having magical blood.

Only this was worse, because I couldn't find out the truth of it - Ezra would have to tell me, and he'd vanished into the night.

Zeb grabbed my hand and pulled me down into his lap, purring against my back.

"It's all right, Gid," Zeb said. "Ezra will be back."

I leaned against him, grateful for his warmth and the hard, muscular chest against me. It felt like Zeb loaning me some certainty or some strength. Ora sat beside Tate, their hand on his arm.

"What... what was all that about?" I asked, finally.

Tate shook his head. "No, not my story to tell. Ezra will tell you as and when he chooses to."

"Oh - of course," I said. "I wouldn't want to pry..."

Although it does feel rather unfair that he should keep secrets when I was so painfully honest.

I bit my lip. Whatever it meant, Tate was right. It wasn't his story to tell, and for all his mystery, I did trust Ezra. I just wished he trusted me enough to be honest with me.

Tate rubbed the heel of his palm into his eye and groaned. "That was fucking stupid of me. But I... no. Never mind. I'm going to get some more ale."

Zeb nibbled on my shoulder where my shirt had fallen back a little, almost absently. I rubbed my fingers over his hand where it rested on my stomach.

Why could none of this be simple?

CHAPTER NINETEEN - IN WHICH GIDEON USES HIS MAGIC INTENTIONALLY

Ora went to swim in the ocean. Tate drank some more and ordered a large piece of apple cake, which he promptly pushed towards me.

"I'm sorry, Gideon," he said.

I looked at the cake and then up at Tate, confused. "Why are you apologising to me?"

"Let's see, this morning you went to talk to a witch and found out an unpleasant truth, and then you came and told all of us about it, which clearly wasn't easy or fun to do." He was ticking off his points on his fingers, which was rather adorable, actually. "We all reassured you, but we haven't had sex about it, and I know that you like to have sex a lot. And you told us that in all likelihood you can feel our emotions, and enhance them, even, and then Ezra and I had a big fight in front of you."

He set his hand down on the table and raised his eyebrows at me. "And besides all that I can see that you're fretting. So, eat some cake, and feel a little bit better, maybe."

The very fact that Tate had considered how the anger was affecting me diminished much of the effect of it. My chest loosened and my stomach stopped knotting itself.

"Thank you, Tate, that's dreadfully kind of you," I said, managing a small smile for him.

Still sitting in Zeb's lap, I leaned forward for the cake and started to eat it, offering forkfuls to Zeb after he cleared his throat expectantly.

Tate was right, the cake, or perhaps, more likely the gesture he made in purchasing the cake for me, did lift my spirits a tad.

We retired to bed soon after. Although Tate was right, and I did like to have sex with my lovers to sort of punctuate an important conversation, I wasn't in the mood that night. The anger lingered at the edges of my mind, and my worry for Ezra was very real.

The notion came to me that he could be picking a fight with someone, or being jumped by pickpockets who could outnumber him kept popping up inside my head, and try as I might I couldn't dispel that.

In bed, Tate fell asleep quite quickly beside me. It was strange to me that he could flare so bright with anger and then let it go just as quickly. His emotions didn't consume him, he could feel it and let it go and go on with his life. I envied him a little for that.

Zeb had insisted on wrapping himself around me on the other side, and although I felt deliciously warm and safe myself, pressed against him and kissing his skin every now and then, even his purr couldn't lull me to sleep.

I closed my eyes and concentrated inside myself instead. The fire within me, the essence of the magic Etta said I had.

Focusing on it as best I could, I tried to tap into the calm and relaxed feelings of Zeb and Tate.

Nothing.

The fire was there, I could feel it curled like a snake inside me, but I couldn't wake it, I couldn't activate it.

I sighed and squirmed out from Zeb's arms.

He grumbled. He never liked me to move once he was

asleep. "It's all right, Zeb," I murmured. "I'm just going to check if Ezra's back."

Zeb opened an eye and regarded me. "Want me to wait with you?"

"You're sweet," I kissed his nose and then his mouth a bit harder. "But no, I'll be alright."

He let go of me so I could climb out and then snuggled up to Tate, both of them soon snoring gently. I looked at them from the edge of the bed and felt the love well up inside me.

That was it. I couldn't focus on emotions I didn't have, I had to use the ones I felt myself.

I let my affection for Zeb and Tate rise to the surface, and then thought about the fire inside - the snake as I'd imagined earlier - and felt it wake for me.

Feeling warm inside and out I leaned over and kissed Zeb's forehead and then Tate's, and fancied that both of them smiled a little in their sleep as I gave them my love.

I have really no idea, no way of knowing, if that was what happened, but I liked to believe it was.

Shaking my head at myself, I pulled my trousers on and slipped out of the room, leaving the door ajar and going next door to knock on Ezra's door.

There was no answer.

I pressed my ear against the wood and listened, but there was no sound from within, no snores or movement at all.

Not back then. Well, what can I do about that?

I had lain awake in bed long enough that the inn was largely quiet now. The sounds of carousing were gone, and although I'm sure there were still plenty of people in their cups, it was a more subdued sort of hour of the night.

All the same, I didn't dare venture down there, alone and unarmed.

So, instead, I thought of what Etta had done. I went back into Tate's room, pulled the door shut and walked to the window, pushing it open and leaning out a little to look up at the moon.

I tried whispering to it - her - Etta had called the moon a her, hadn't she?

"Uh, excuse me," I started. "But I'd really like to uh…" what was I thinking? What was I trying to do? I wanted Ezra, that's all I knew. Etta hadn't said anything about being able to summon people, but she had said there'd be a protection and that implied some kind of link didn't it?

I thought about the love I had for him, felt the fire inside me and gazed at the three quarter moon.

"I'd like to find Ezra, uh, to know he's all right. Can you please bring him safely back to me?"

I looked down at the ground, a floor below us, and saw someone pissing against the wall opposite.

This was ridiculous. What did I think I was doing?

I'd found out I had some fae blood and now I was asking the moon for favours?

Ridiculous. I could practically hear my father scoffing at my foolishness.

I pulled the window shut and drew the thin curtain across it, looked back at the shapes in the bed and climbed in beside them. I felt weary, or possibly just weary of myself and my own foolishness.

I fell asleep.

I woke to a knock on the door and hurried over to open it.

Ezra stood in the hallway. The pain in my chest loosened and I smiled in relief.

"Gideon, are you… are you all right?" he asked. He looked me up and down and looked past me to the sleeping forms of Zeb and Tate.

"Yes, I'm all right," I said. "I'm glad to see you back here, though."

"Why don't you come into my room?" He nodded down the hallway.

I closed the door behind me and followed him into his room.

He lit the lantern and sat down on the bed, looking down at the floor as he pulled his boots off. "Gideon, did you... did you do something?"

I licked my lips, uncertain of what to do. It felt too presumptuous somehow to sit beside him, so I sat on a chair near the bed, facing him.

"I don't know if I did," I said. "I tried something, but I had no idea what I was doing... I didn't think it would work." I closed my eyes. Trying to speak to the moon seemed more like a dream than a thing I'd actually done.

"Well." Ezra set his boots to the side and shrugged off his jacket and tossed it to me. "Hang this up will you?"

I obeyed without thinking about it, setting his jacket on the hook on the back of the door. "You came back to the inn looking for me?" I asked.

"Aye, I had a clear image of you," he said. He patted the mattress beside him and I sat, although not too close. My heart was fluttering in my chest like a trapped songbird.

"You did?"

"Mm," he said. He sighed heavily. "Listen, you know I have a certain distrust of magic of all kinds, but... this?"

I swallowed a lump in my throat, afraid that this was him telling me it was too much, that he couldn't be with me after all.

"Yes?" I asked, as he seemed lost in his thoughts, and the anticipation was killing me.

"This was different," he said, finally. His voice lacked the usual hard edge, and it was more like Zeb's purr than Ezra's usual growl. He stripped off his black linen shirt. "This felt like a pleasant waking dream. Like being called home at the end of a long day by someone who loves me."

"But... but that's not bad at all," I said, breathless with relief.

Ezra grinned at me, wolfish as ever.

"No, it's not." He put his hand on my thigh and sighed again. "I reckon I owe you an explanation, but perhaps you'll let it sit until morning? I'd rather tell the story just once, with Ora and Zeb to hear. And I reckon I owe the captain an apology as well."

I bit my lip to stop the beaming smile that was threatening. I didn't stop myself throwing my arms around him and he laughed, and fell back on the bed, pulling me with him.

"Fuck, Gideon, what've you done to me?" He pushed his nose against my neck and huffed a little.

"I hope only good things," I said, feeling giddy with the release of fear.

"Maybe so," he said.

I pushed myself up on my hands and cleared my throat, remembering that he preferred to sleep alone.

"I guess I'd best get back to the other room, although... I suppose the door is locked now..."

Ezra reached up and tugged on a lock of my hair gently. His eyes had gone liquid, dark and deep and entrancing. "May as well stay here with me," he said.

I let myself smile as wide as I wished to as he pulled me in against him and we kissed as if we would never stop.

CHAPTER TWENTY - IN WHICH GIDEON'S LOVERS HAVE SEX ABOUT IT ALL

I woke up lying on my side with my head on Ezra's shoulder and my back pressed against his side. His arm curled around me, fingertips barely grazing my stomach.

I lay still, inhaling the musky, leather tinged smell of him and feeling content. The best mornings were of course, when I woke up with all my lovers together, but this had to be a close second. Ezra, for whatever he was hiding, had accepted my magic, and allowed me to sleep with him.

I hummed happily, thinking of how hopefully, later we would all be together. And perhaps, some time later still Ezra would put his collar on me and we could try another round of training. The thought made my cock twitch and I smiled, turning my head to kiss at the skin of Ezra's arm.

He sighed in his sleep, a pleasant, gentle sound that went right to my heart.

I lay and dreamed a little, thinking of that house I had conjured up, with a herb garden for Ora and a ... well, it was a dungeon, wasn't it? For Ezra. The five of us living in peace, unafraid of anyone chasing us down. It was such a pleasant dream.

Ezra shifted behind me, turned over, so his chest and hard

cock were pressed against me, barely concealed by the thin fabric of his undergarments. His other hand moved to caress my chest.

I moaned, instantly hard myself, flooded with joy from the image of the house and a happy life with my lovers. Ezra's face nuzzled at the back of my neck and then I felt teeth sink into my skin.

"Good morning," I said, breathless, and tipped my head forward a little so he could access more of my skin.

"Mornin'" he rumbled against my spine. He ground his hardness against my rear and I pushed back against him as best I could. Every inch of my skin was instantly on alert and anticipating what he was doing with his hands.

There was a knock at the door and both of us stilled.

Ezra sighed. "Did you summon someone else, pet?"

"I don't... I don't think so," I said, pulling away from him a little so I didn't just impale myself on him and ignore the door.

"We're not done," he murmured in my ear, making me shiver.

Then Ezra got out of bed, pulled his trousers on and opened the door a crack. Ora was there, smiling wide.

"Good morning!" They said, very cheerful. "I went next door to see Gideon but I guess he's in here?"

"I am," I waved.

"Wonderful, Tate and Zeb are awake, too," Ora said. "Are we all calm now? Can we talk without yelling?"

Ezra groaned and scratched the back of his neck. "Aye, probably. But you are interrupting something."

I slid out of the bed and pulled my shirt on. Although I did feel somewhat on edge and deprived, if we could all talk and Tate and Ezra could make peace then maybe we could all enjoy each other afterwards.

Ezra watched me and sighed. "Right." He picked up his own shirt and the two of us followed Ora out of the room and into

Tate's, where he was shaving around his goatee. Zeb was lying on the bed, watching him. He looked over and his face brightened when he saw me and I waved.

"Right, Ezra," Tate said. He wiped the last shaving soap off his face with a towel and reached his hand out to him. "I'm sorry, I was totally out of line last night. Nothing can justify what I said."

Ezra took a deep breath, and standing next to him I felt a wave of irritation emanating from him. I took his hand and tried to think about the calm contentment I'd felt in bed that morning. The serenity of being in his arms. I hoped I could give some of that back to him.

Finally he took Tate's hand and shook it.

"Thank you," Ezra said, a little stiffly. "I overreacted too, I reckon. And, well, if we're all of us going to do this and stick with Gideon and with each other, then you ought to know that I have a wife in India."

I coughed, a little startled, but proud of Ezra for sharing.

Ora sat on the bed beside Zeb and started to stroke his bare back, Tate leaned against the wall beside the looking glass and I stayed beside Ezra, squeezing his hand and focusing as much as I could on my love for him. I hoped it gave him strength somehow.

"Arranged marriage. Neither of us wanted it, but I was set to inherit her family house, the land near Bengal, if we married. She would inherit nothing, and if I didn't marry I wouldn't inherit my family's money either. While visiting, I discovered her love for her handmaiden, and we negotiated a deal." Ezra looked at me and then at the others, his expression blank but for some fear in his eyes. I nodded.

"Go on," Tate said.

"We married, she took the house and lives in comfort with as many handmaidens as she likes, and I disappeared. On business, officially, to keep our parents happy. I write to her, she writes to me, and I send money when she needs it, but the arrangement suits us both."

I breathed out slowly.

The room was silent for a moment. Zeb sat up and shrugged. "I have wives too."

"You have cats," Ora said, grinning.

"Well. They used to be my wives," Zeb said. "Now I have you." He wrapped his arms around Ora and showered kisses over their face until they giggled.

"Is it all right?" Ezra asked me, half turning to me.

I nodded, because although it did feel strange to imagine Ezra pledging his undying love to a woman, I knew it wouldn't change anything between us.

"Yes, if you can accept my magic, then of course. I can't... I can't picture you getting married, let alone to a woman, but I understand."

Tate grinned, crossed the room and hugged Ezra tight. Ezra stiffened for the briefest moment and then returned it, burying his face into Tate's shoulder.

I breathed in, relief and joy flooding my blood as my lovers showed each other their love.

I can feel it. I can feel their love, their happiness, their relief that we're all together... I can feel their love for me, too.

I tipped my head back and silently thanked the moon, and my mother, and whoever was listening for these men in my life.

A hand grabbed mine and Zeb yanked me onto the bed so I crashed into him and Ora. Ora tugged my shirt off and Zeb's hands found the waistband of my trousers. I laughed, trying to steady myself but it was impossible, balanced on their tangled limbs as they moved and tugged at me.

I stole a kiss from Zeb's lips when the opportunity presented itself. Ora's hand closed on my cock - which was quick to harden after my moments with Ezra in bed earlier.

The mattress shifted and I looked over to see Tate, pushed

on his back with Ezra over him, pulling his shirt off and hands stroking over his chest.

"So beautiful," I murmured. My love welled up in me again, and now I was here with my lovers and I could connect them all together again.

Ora hummed. "I feel it," they said, nuzzling into the hair at the back of my neck. "Your magic, it's making every touch more intense."

Zeb tugged me by the hips so I was between his legs. His finger moved back to tease himself open. I moaned and pushed my own rear towards Ora, who wrapped an arm around my waist and pressed their cock against me.

Ezra and Tate moved closer to us. Ezra had Tate's wrists pinned over his head, and my heart ached with need. I reached a hand past Zeb to place it on Tate's chest, feeling the rise and fall of his quick breathes as he gave himself to Ezra. The truest possible apology, perhaps. His face was lit with a soft smile, looking at me with true love, and then back at Ezra, licking his lips.

I wanted to be everywhere at once, experiencing everything. My desire inflamed me, and I gave into it, moaning as Zeb guided me inside him.

Behind me, Ora moved and I felt them teasing at my hole with the slick silk of their cock.

"Yes, please, please..." I moaned. "I want all of you..."

"Greedy, pet," Ezra growled. He'd stripped off his trousers at some point and positioned himself on Tate's chest, letting him lick at his cock. Ezra's hand found my hair, fisted, pulled on the strands close to the roots and I groaned my response.

Ora's chest was flush to my back and I felt them tilt their chin up to nibble at Ezra's arm. Zeb lay back, his head on Tate's shoulder, his hand fisting Tate's cock.

We were all connected. The flames of my magic filled me

with warm sparks of light, and with one deep breath, I let it flood out of me and into each of my beloved lovers.

Tate groaned, bucked against Ezra and took his cock deep into his mouth. I watched, feeling my cock pulse inside Zeb.

Zeb's hand closed on my jaw, tugging me slightly forward - for with Ezra's hand in my hair I couldn't move my head further - and I lost myself in a hot kiss. Zeb's tongue flicked against mine, tempting my mouth open and I gave him that easily, feeling even there, the flow of energy that felt not at all like a taking or feeding off of their energy.

It was more like I was feeding them, that I was sharing something essential of myself with each of them in the best, most delicious way possible. But in doing so I wasn't losing myself, it felt like I was sharing from an endless well.

Zeb made a sound deep in his throat that was almost a yowl. The hand I had been trying to use to balance closed around his cock and I pumped it, encouraging him on.

Behind me, Ora bit deep into my shoulder and I gasped, back arching. Ezra's hand in my hair caused a million more points of sparkling pain as I yanked against him.

It was delicious. My gasp melted into a moan as Ora shoved deep inside me, clinging around my waist so hard it was almost painful there as well, but I found myself revelling in it.

"For the love of..." Ezra dropped his hand out of my hair and I glanced at him, saw his expression dark with lust as he pulled Tate's legs up and shoved inside him.

Both of them groaned together and I felt it like an echo of my own need reverberating through my bones. My hand had been knocked off Tate's chest but now, as Ezra started to pound him, Tate took it and threaded our fingers together. He brought my hand to his mouth and kissed the back of it, his breath puffing against my skin.

"Fuck, please," Tate groaned. "It's so good, Gid..."

I didn't even question Tate giving me credit for his pleasure when it was Ezra inside him. It made perfect sense. All our pleasure was shared, a river of golden light flowing between and into all of us, amplifying itself.

Ezra moaned as well and, as if we had planned it, all of us breathed in at the same moment, bucked our bodies and orgasmed in unison. The golden fire sparked and cracked, searing my skin from within as it fed itself off all the reflected ecstasy.

Ezra bucked again, Ora filled me, buried deep inside and I felt myself squeezed dry by Zeb's body clenching. Tate was a moaning wreck, half buried under Ezra and Zeb, hands stroking him all over.

It took a few moments before the golden light cleared, and each of us slowly shifted, disentangling ourselves only enough to collapse into a mess of limbs. A pile of hot, satisfied bodies all still trying to touch each other and share kisses.

After a good few minutes, Tate cleared his throat. His voice was muffled but whether it was from skin or bedclothes I had no clue.

"Well, Ora," he asked, lazily, his voice barely containing a laugh. "Did Gideon feed off our souls or our life force?"

"No," Ora said. I felt lips move against my shoulder blade and reached to squeeze Ora's hip. "No, he *gave*... he gave us more I think. I think it made everything more... so much more intense."

"I felt that too," Zeb said. I tipped my head to look at him, realised I had my head on his chest. His black pointed cat ears were poking through his hair.

"So did we all," Ezra said. I felt his hand in my hair again but this time it was a gentle ruffle, the way you might pet a dog. "Good work, pet."

CHAPTER TWENTY-ONE - IN WHICH DECISIONS ARE MADE

"I had a dream," I said, slowly, after everyone had been lying together for a few more minutes.

Tate tensed and tried to sit up, rolling Zeb a little more onto me. "With Solomon again?"

"No, not like that," I said. "It was a few days ago, actually, but I was shy about it."

"You? Shy? I thought we'd fucked that out of you." Ezra found my thigh with his fingers and pinched it, making me yelp. I blushed at his words, but couldn't deny them. Tate chuckled and shifted, moving up against the pillows, Ora tugged me a bit more off Zeb and we all resettled together, more comfortably.

"Tell us your dream," Zeb said. His voice was rich with contentment and I predicted he'd be asleep again very soon.

"Uh, well, this one was about the future." I started, cleared my throat and plunged on. "In it, we had a house together somewhere, it was overlooking the ocean and there was a garden and a big verandah... all of us living there together, happy and safe."

Ora hummed and nuzzled my shoulder. "Yeah? Close to the water though?"

"I think so, I think we were just sort of... up a path from a beach with a harbour. Up on the hill so we could see ships coming and going." I reached up to caress Zeb's jaw with my fingers. "Ezra was building a sort of sex playroom in the basement."

Ezra chuckled. "You can put a wager on that, if I were to settle down, I'd want a playroom."

He nudged me with his elbow and I grinned at him, feeling the heat stir in me just from the promise in his look.

I looked at Tate next and his expression was pensive.

"It's a nice dream, lad," he said. "But until we shake your father and the Royal Fleet I don't see how it could come to be. And besides, we'd need a few good years of pirating before we could afford such a thing."

"Couple of Spanish Treasure Ships," Ezra added.

"Would you consider it?" I asked. "I know you both love the sea, and the freedom it affords you, to settle on land is so different, a different life."

Tate shrugged and then laughed good naturedly. "If meeting you has taught me nothing else, Gideon, it's taught me I'll consider anything."

I flushed with happiness. That was good enough for me. The possibility of such a future at some point was delightful.

"So, Captain," Ezra said. "What's the immediate plan for the Grey Kelpie?"

Tate looked at him, tipped his eyes up to the ceiling and sighed. "The New World, as you said, it's the last place they'll expect us to go."

Ezra smiled softly, and nodded once.

Zeb yawned, turned over and started snoring.

"How long until we make sail?" Ora asked, stretching over me to stroke Tate's arm.

"One more day here, let the crew unwind before we go. We'll need to stock up on supplies..." Tate looked at me. "I'll leave those calculations to you, if you don't mind, Gid?"

"That's fine, it is my job after all," I said, smiling. "I'll head to the ship and see what we need."

"And Ezra and I will chart the course," Tate said. "Be back on the ship at sundown and we'll sail out on the next tide after that."

The day was a pleasant one. I spent the morning going through our stocks, checking what we'd need for the coming voyage and making a list of needed supplies, which I took to Sagorika. She sent Zack and Anton to purchase the supplies and load them into the ship's stores.

Then I spent the afternoon wandering the streets with Zeb and Ora and taking in the sights.

We were debating whether or not to visit with another witch, when Tate found us.

"I just want to see what they have to say about Zeb's shapeshifting," Ora said. "You never know, it might be useful."

"We know we can trust Etta," I said. "But not any of the others, it's too dangerous to just go into one of those stores at random."

"I know all I need to know about my shapeshifting," Zeb said. "I'm fine."

"What if the spell wears off?" Ora said, exasperated. "You might be trapped as a human, or a cat!"

Tate walked around the corner and spotted us. "There you are!"

"Here we are," I said, relieved to be interrupted in this case. "Please tell Ora the witches aren't safe?"

"I'll tell all of you that, and that you need to get to the ship," he said. I looked at the sky, checking the position of the sun, it was high still.

"It's still afternoon, I thought you said we had until sundown."

"That was before the rumours started up at the Mad Parrot that the Navy is snooping around these waters," Tate said.

A chill cooled my veins and I nodded, taking Ora's hand. "Right, to the ship then."

"Is anyone else from the ship missing?" Zeb asked. "I can find them."

"Just Zack," Tate said. "Please, if you can find him and bring him to the dock, Zeb."

Zeb promptly shifted into cat form and bounded away, sniffing the air.

Within a half hour, Zack and Zeb climbed the gangplank and we cast off from Nassau.

"Sorry, Captain," Zack said, as the sails filled with wind. "I was just... Uh, busy. With a watch. I mean, a witch. I was seeing a witch."

Tate shrugged. "Your business is your own, lad." He went to take the helm from Ezra.

Zack smiled at me and hurried to my side. He leaned in and whispered. "I went to see the one Sagorika suggested for you, she's very good isn't she?"

"Yes, she was helpful, if... fond of blood," I said.

I didn't want to pry, but Zack looked so excited and was biting his lip. "Do you want to know what she did?" he asked.

"Sure, if you don't mind telling me," I said. Zack took my arm companionably and we walked to my old cabin, where Zack bunked now.

"I told her about my, well, you know. My gender and my body and all, and she's given me a charm to stop the monthlies, and she said if I keep on wearing it, within a few months my voice will deepen and I can maybe even grow a beard!"

My eyes widened and my breath caught. I couldn't imagine

better news for Zack. "That's wonderful, really, Zack. I'm so happy for you." I gave him a hug, which he returned happily.

"The rest will require a stronger spell," he said. "But honestly, I'm over the moon with excitement." He sat back on the bed, resting on his hands and beamed at me. "Thank you Gideon, I never thought I could be this happy."

"I don't think I did anything," I said. "But you're welcome."

"You showed me it's alright to be myself, and to accept myself," he said.

I flushed a little. "Well, that was simple enough. I'm pleased. Now, uh, promise you won't be afraid if I tell you what the witch told me?"

Zack nodded. I filled him in on the basics of what I knew. His smile faded a little, but he didn't appear to be afraid. Finally, he snapped his fingers, his face brightening.

"It's just like the story I told on the beach!" He said. "The one about kelpies. One of your great-great-grandmothers or someone must've got pregnant to an incubus!"

My eyes widened a little but I nodded. "Yes, yes, it seems so," I said.

We sailed until clouds covered the moon and visibility was wrecked - soon into the second watch of the night. We made anchor and I slept warm in Tate's arms, Ezra on the other side of me and Zeb on the other side of Tate. Ora took their customary sleeping spot in the netting under the bowsprit, but the very gesture of Ezra bedding down with us filled me with joy.

The next morning we were awakened before dawn by the sound of the alarm bell. Tate and Ezra leapt into action, and pulled on clothes. I was fast on their heels, and even Zeb trailed out of the cabin.

"Sails on the horizon!" Sagorika said and pointed to the North. "Navy must've come around, somehow."

"Then we sail South," Tate said. "Try and lose them. If we're lucky they won't have recognised us. Zeb, get up into the crow's nest, you've the best eyes."

"Yeah, yeah," Zeb said, and nimbly climbed the rigging. His black tail sprouting to give him better balance as he scaled the main mast to the top most point.

The next few days were tense. The sails on the horizon seemed to follow us, and from what we could make out through the spyglass they were definitely British.

They would sometimes get closer, and sometimes we thought we'd lost them, but then the next morning, or a few hours later they'd be back again.

On the fourth day, Ezra brought the map to Tate as he manned the helm. I was beside him, watching the way his arms moved as he gripped the wheel. It was positively hypnotic. I had lost many minutes to watching his body.

"What've you found, Ezra?" Tate asked, barely glancing at the map.

"Just charting our course since we left Nassau. We need to go further West if we're aiming to land in the Americas."

Tate looked at the chart properly then, and sighed. "We don't have a choice, Ez. You've seen the sails, same as the rest of us, we have to keep evading them."

"Starting to feel like we're being shepherded," Ezra grumbled.

"To where?" I asked. I looked over his shoulders at the map.

Ezra shrugged. "I think it could be to Kingston, look." He sketched a trajectory from where we were towards Kingston - due South. "Thornton wanted us there, and maybe your father..."

"Well, I'm open to suggestions," Tate said. "But they're too close for us to try and hide."

. . .

So the game of chase continued, and the next day it became very clear they were indeed shepherding us towards Kingston.

"There's only one other option," Tate said. He'd gathered Ezra, Sagorika and me in his cabin to discuss what to do. "The Splintered Isles. We know they won't follow us there."

Sagorika whistled. "It's an awfully big risk, Tate."

"I'm aware, but it's that or sail into Kingston and be captured instantly by Gideon's father's men, and we know how that ends up for all of us."

I felt the cold pang of guilt in my chest and sighed deeply.

"We can't do that," I said. "It's out of the question. I think we should go to the Splintered Isles."

"I agree with Gid," Ezra said. He folded his arms over his chest. "I think we should take our chances at the Isles."

The air was tense as Sagorika looked around the faces gathered. She pursed her lips and exhaled through her nose, before finally nodding. "Aye, it's our best bet."

"Which means we need to adjust course now," Tate said, tiredly. "I'll take the helm."

Sagorika pulled her hair back into a loose knot and sighed deeply.

"I'll alert the crew, we can't have another Joseph. I'll let them know that... maybe things will turn up in their dreams that shouldn't be there." She turned on her heel and left the cabin, skirts swishing around her legs.

"None of you have had dreams about Solomon, have you?" I asked, looking between Ezra and Tate, they both shook their heads.

"You'll know if I do," Tate said. "I'll wake up screaming."

"I'll see if there's any kind of protection Ora can put on the ship."

I felt a terrible sense of dread, and hoped the others couldn't sense it on me. The last thing we needed was for the Navy to chase us into Solomon's clutches. I had no doubt he'd kill the crew of the ship outright... But as for myself and Tate, that would be a different story.

Tate he wanted to torture, and me? He'd known I had some power, but surely now that I understood it myself, he would understand it fully.

An ill-divining part of my soul imagined him using this powers to sway me, to plumb the depths of my incubus heritage and make me into a weapon. Control my mind and make me enjoy it or some other horrible thing like that.

I worried at my fingernails as Tate went to the helm. After a moment, I went to find Ora and talk magic.

CHAPTER TWENTY-TWO - IN WHICH PLANS PLAY OUT AS THEY SHOULD

THE SPLINTERED ISLES

The waves lapped at the rocks and Solomon pressed his finger to the sharpest point, hissing as it pierced his skin. He allowed a drop of blood to drip into the waves and watched as it dissolved into the water.

Then he pressed the tiny wound against the knotted cord he held. So many knots, each one with a distinct purpose, each holding some tiny bit of Solomon's will.

He sniffed the breeze and it was almost as if he could taste the Grey Kelpie's approach. Scenting Tate on the wind like a bloodhound.

"It won't be long now," he said to the waves, pleased. "After so many delays, so many times I almost had him and was thwarted…"

Remembering wasn't pleasant, but Solomon did it anyway.

The Trinity Royal had come so close, they'd had Tate in chains in their brig… but then somehow the damned crew had broken out and freed them. Thornton had earned Solomon's wrath for that and he was still paying him back with nightmares.

Thornton had been well on the way to delivering Tate to

him, and then he'd slipped through his fingers and Solomon was left scrying the horizon, searching once more for that ship.

Something - someone - had shielded the ship from his reach.

He hadn't been able to reach into Gideon's dreams since that one fateful night when they had met in a dream of Thornton's. Gideon had almost succumbed to him then, but he'd slipped away. Like trying to hold onto lightning. And he'd felt his little jinx evaporate before it could incapacitate the annoying pup.

"*Gideon*," he hissed, his voice full of venom.

Solomon glanced up at the sky and licked his lips. Thinking about that night made him hungry for blood.

But he took some solace in the knowledge they were closer now. Chased towards him by visions, illusions of ships Solomon conjured from the mist. The knots in the cord maintained them - made them look real, made them look like they were closing in, forcing the Kelpie towards Solomon.

And of course, after their run in with Thornton, no one on that ship wished to let the ships close enough to see they were merely tricks.

They ran as a rabbit would, right into the snare Solomon had laid out so carefully before them.

He sniffed the air again. *Closer, still.*

Soon, soon I will have my hands-on Tate again and I'll make him pay for each minute I've spent here alone.

In fact, was that a sail on the horizon now? It was distant, but... yes. A sail. A sail he knew very well indeed.

Solomon stood, waded into the waves until he was waist deep and let the magical energy of the islands flow into him. All it would take was one pull and the tides and the wind would bring the ship to him.

What was he waiting for? He clenched his fist and *pulled.*

To be continued...

Keep a weather eye out for His Piratical Harem book four:
Captain's Treasure

If you enjoyed this book, please consider leaving a review on
Amazon. Indie authors rely on star ratings and reviews to go up
the algorithm and be seen by more readers.

Sign up for Drake's newsletter for updates on new releases
https://www.subscribepage.com/q4c4n0
Come join Drake's Crew reader's group to meet other fans and
get exclusive content. Maybe you'll even get to name – or
become! – a character in the next book
https://www.facebook.com/groups/1272511269588779/

Find Drake online:

Twitter: https://twitter.com/DrakeLamarque

Pinterest: https://www.pinterest.nz/drakelamarque/

Newsletter: https://www.subscribepage.com/q4c4n0

BookBub: https://www.bookbub.com/profile/drake-lamarque

Instagram: https://www.instagram.com/drakelamarque/

This book would not be what it is without my incredible demon, my partner in ridiculousness, alpha reader and proofer. You're awesome and I have too many nicknames for you, so let's just go with you're the Tate to my Gideon. Love you always.

To my beta-reader, thanks for all your work, your attention to detail and realising when there's a big gaping plot hole because something which was clear in my head didn't make it to the page. You rock. Many sleepy Zeb snuggles for you.

And finally to all my readers, thanks for buying the book and for showing your support. Especially to the readers in Drake's Crew. A twenty-one gun salute to all of you.

Buy Now

I've never been what I was supposed to be. Wealthy sons of Port Governors aren't supposed to be ejected from the British Navy after less than a year, they're not supposed to like pulp romances or daydream about the handsome heroes of the stories instead of the heroines.

When my Father issued me an order to marry a woman, I knew I had no choice but to make my own way in the world, and I found a berth on the first ship out of Jamaica.

I didn't mean to join a pirate ship, and I certainly didn't intend to find myself the cabin boy to an incredibly charming Pirate Captain. Or that I'd also be attracted to the mysterious First Mate, or that both of them would show me all sorts of unspeakable and salacious pleasures while on board. How can I choose just one of them when I want both?

In addition to confusion on board the ship, there's also enchanting genderfluid merfolk, a cat which seems to understand a lot more than it should, an unseasonable storm and a sea witch with a serious grudge... and with all these complications, I am definitely in over my head.

--

Come and meet the crew:

Gideon: an innocent with a lot of forbidden desires and a lot of love to give

Tate: a huge, muscular ship's captain with a sweet side

Ezra: a dominant and closed off first mate

Ora: a genderqueer, curious and affectionate merman

BOOK TWO OF HIS PIRATICAL HAREM – FIRST MATE'S PET

Buy Now

Things were looking good, until the ship's cat became a man...

I didn't mean to join a pirate ship, but now that I'm here, well. Life is pretty good. Between the sexy and intimidating Captain Tate, the mysterious First Mate, Ora the merfolk and now Zeb the ship's cat I'm well entertained.

Rumours abound that the Royal Navy are searching for me at my father's order, and between that, an eventful trip to Tortuga (the famed pirate town) and maintaining the relationships with the crew... I've certainly got my work cut out for me.

Meet the crew:

Gideon: a well bred young man who is discovering his forbidden desires aren't necessarily a problem at sea
    Tate: the impressive Captain with a sweet side
    Ezra: the controlling and alluring First Mate

Ora: a genderqueer, sweet and mystical merman
Zeb: a cat shifter, who's learning about being human

MM romance, this is part two of a multiple book series -
working towards a HEA at the end of the series

Rival Princes by Jaxon Knight

There are three golden rules for new recruits at Fairyland
Theme Park:

1. No breaking character, even if you're dying of heat exhaustion
    2. Always give guests the most magical time
    3. No falling in love.

Nate's only been at work one day, and he's already broken all
three.

Fast-tracked into a Prince role, Nate's at odds with Dash, the
handsome not-so-charming prince who is supposed to be
training him. Nate doesn't know how he ended up on Dash's bad
side, but the broody prince sure is hot when he gets mad.

Dash has worked long and hard to play Prince Justice at
Fairyland. Now, instead of focusing on his own performance, he
is forced to train newbie Nate to be the perfect prince. Nate's
annoying ease with the guests coupled with his charm and good

looks could dethrone Dash from his number one spot ... so why does he secretly want to kiss him?

Fairyland heats up as sparks fly between the two rival princes. Will they get their fairytale romance before they're kicked out of Fairyland for good?

Find out in this standalone MM contemporary romance by Jaxon Knight, set in an amusement park where fairytales can come true.

Mischief and Mayhem by Jaxon Knight

Mischief

Protecting royalty at Fairyland theme park seemed about as far from Afghanistan as Cody could get. But the hot new rollercoaster brings up some unexpected trouble - and not the kind of trouble he knows how to handle alone.

Mayhem

Dean loves running the Spaceship Mayhem roller coaster - he gets to meet new people every day! When he sees a handsome, troubled security guard repeatedly fail to ride it, he sees an opportunity to help. And maybe they can be more than friends?

Cody reluctantly accepts cute, boy-next-door Dean's help and sparks fly between them, but between mischief, mayhem and miscommunication, can they ever make a relationship work?

Mischief and Mayhem is a slow burn, opposites attract MM

sweet romance featuring snark, foolishness, motorbikes, assumptions, the chicken door and a HEA

Recipe for Chaos by Jaxon Knight

The recipe is simple:
    Charlie cooks an amazing meal
    Charlie impresses heir to the theme park Max Jones
    Charlie gets a promotion and a dash of control over his
kitchen

But the perfect recipe becomes unpalatable with one wrong
ingredient and Max Jones is not behaving how Charlie
expected...

Max is meant to inherit the entire Fairyland theme park but he
just wants to party, have fun and bed as many people as possible.
That is, until he meets Charlie and falls for him so hard he can't
even finish the delicious meal.

Charlie doesn't have time for clubs or helicopter flights over the
city, but Max is accustomed to getting what he wants, and he
wants Charlie.

Featuring one part Billionaire, one part sensible chef, six cups of attraction, a generous dose of snark and a freshly prepared Happy Ever After.

The Good, the Bad, and the Dad by Jaxon Knight

Haru is a single dad, a widower, doing his best to balance his career and raising his little girl, Minako. Thankfully Fairyland theme park is a haven for both of them. However, when both a prince and a pirate start courting Haru, his balancing act gets a lot harder...

Cillian plays a pirate at Fairyland theme park and he loves playing the rogueish character in and out of work hours. The last thing he wants is to settle down with a guy with a kid, so can't he stop thinking about handsome single dad Haru. And why can't he stop looking at pictures of Prince Magnificence and his stupid symmetrical face? And why does he keep running into both of them?

Grayson feels he's found his home in the role of Prince Magnificence, but he's more likely to run from love than seek it out. Until he meets Haru, that is. Christmas is complicated by Grayson's role being featured in a special Christmas celebration. Not only that, but his feelings for Haru, and his possible rival

Cillian keep on growing. Maybe it's time to stop hiding who he really is?

--

The Good, the Bad and the Dad is a sweet MMM romance featuring a single father, a rogue and a trans prince with a heart of gold. No cheating, just the tentative first steps into polyamory.